THE MAHABHARATA

More classic literature available
from Macmillan Collector's Library

The Ramayana by Valmiki

The Odyssey by Homer

The Iliad by Homer

The Aeneid by Virgil

Fairies, Elves and Sprites

Mermaids, Sirens and Selkies

Witches, Wizards and Sorcerers

Dragons, Wyverns and Serpents

Greek Myths: Gods and Goddesses

Greek Myths: Heroes and Heroines

VYASA

THE MAHABHARATA

Translated by
ROMESH C. DUTT

With an introduction by
ARSHIA SATTAR

MACMILLAN COLLECTOR'S LIBRARY

This translation first published 1910

This edition first published 2025 by Macmillan Collector's Library
an imprint of Pan Macmillan
The Smithson, 6 Briset Street, London EC1M 5NR
EU representative: Macmillan Publishers Ireland Ltd,
1st Floor, The Liffey Trust Centre, 117–126 Sheriff Street Upper,
Dublin 1, DO1 YC43
Associated companies throughout the world
www.panmacmillan.com

ISBN 978-1-0350-4853-3

Introduction and Character List copyright © Arshia Sattar 2025

All rights reserved. No part of this publication may be reproduced,
stored in a retrieval system, or transmitted, in any form, or by any means
(electronic, mechanical, photocopying, recording or otherwise)
without the prior written permission of the publisher.

1 3 5 7 9 8 6 4 2

A CIP catalogue record for this book is available from the British Library.

Endpaper pattern by Andrew Davidson
Typeset in Plantin by Jouve (UK), Milton Keynes
Printed and bound in China by Imago

This book is sold subject to the condition that it shall not, by way of
trade or otherwise, be lent, hired out, or otherwise circulated without the
publisher's prior consent in any form of binding or cover other than that
in which it is published and without a similar condition including
this condition being imposed on the subsequent purchaser.

Visit **www.panmacmillan.com** to read more
about all our books and to buy them.

Contents

Introduction vii

Character List xvii

THE MAHABHARATA

I. Astra Darsana (*The Tournament*) 3

II. Swayamvara (*The Bride's Choice*) 31

III. Rajasuya (*The Imperial Sacrifice*) 63

IV. Dyuta (*The Fatal Dice*) 95

V. Pativrata-Mahatmya (*Woman's Love*) 125

VI. Go-Harana (*Cattle-Lifting*) 167

VII. Udyoga (*The Council of War*) 199

VIII. Bhishma-Badha (*Fall of Bhishma*) 233

IX. Drona-Badha (*Fall of Drona*) 279

X. Karna-Badha (*Fall of Karna*) 321

XI. Sraddha (*Funeral Rites*) 357

XII. Aswa-Medha (*Sacrifice of the Horse*) 381

Conclusion 403

Glossary 409

Introduction

ARSHIA SATTAR

'What is found here may be found elsewhere, but what is not found here cannot be found anywhere,' the *Mahabharata* says about itself. This immodest claim becomes less incredible when we consider that the text is seven times longer than the *Iliad* and the *Odyssey* put together and its definitive Sanskrit text took teams of scholars nearly fifty years to compile.

Attributed to the sage Vyasa, the *Mahabharata* is 100,000 verses in length and belongs, in its earliest narrative layer, to the bardic tradition of oral composition. One of the two great epics of Hinduism, the *Mahabharata* was recited and re-recited over centuries, each bard adding and expanding the parts he loved best, minimizing or excising the parts he did not like as much, modifying episodes and characters to reflect the times in which he made his poetry.

Composed as it was over centuries by many differing minds and many competing voices, the

INTRODUCTION

Mahabharata has hundreds of characters, thousands of stories and it explores complex moral issues. You might well ask why, two thousand five hundred years later, we should read a text from a time and a place that no longer exist in a language that is no longer spoken. Quite simply because the *Mahabharata* is one of the greatest stories ever told. We read it still because the moral dilemmas it confronts make us stop and think about ourselves in our own time and place – dilemmas of duty to others and responsibility to oneself, the conflict between righteousness and justice, the relationship between war and other kinds of sanctioned violence, the desire for power and the quest for truth – these are questions that we still ask, answers that we still seek, no matter who we are or where we might be in the world.

The *Mahabharata*'s sister text in ancient India is the *Ramayana*, also composed around the same time. The Hindu epics, as they are commonly described, share concerns and anxieties, aspirations and ideals. Both revolve around the crucial idea of righteous kingship – not simply who will be king, but who should be king. The protagonists of both texts, Rama in the *Ramayana* and Yudhishthir in the *Mahabharata*, are deprived of their rightful inheritance, sent into exile and must fight a war before they can return to reclaim their patrimony. Each of them returns with a better sense of who they are and what they must do in order to fulfil their destiny as warriors and kings. Their time in the forest led them to conversations with sages and wise men, but they also had hostile encounters with strange and monstrous beings. Each has to consider what it means to be a warrior and to embrace the idea of violence as an integral part of the code that he must live by; each has been intellectually, emotionally and morally challenged by those closest to him – by a wife, by a brother.

Although the stories celebrate a profoundly masculinist universe, the women stand at the throbbing heart of the action in the *Mahabharata*. They appear primarily as wives and mothers, separated from their natal homes and, therefore, already more vulnerable. However, they surprise us in their determined quest for power, in their burning desire to avenge what has been done to them, and in the individual agency that they wrest from the patriarchy that surrounds them. The challenges they pose strike at the ethical foundations of a society that sees women as fundamentally less worthy than men. Women are the first to question both the individual morality and the public ethics of their husbands and family elders in the epic

INTRODUCTION

and, in doing so, they allow us to examine what, if anything, has changed over millennia of systemic misogyny.

Despite the welter of myths and tales and branching narratives in this massive text, the central story of the *Mahabharata* is strong and clear. It concerns a ruling family and their disputed throne, claimed with equal conviction by two sets of cousins, the five Pandavs and the one hundred Kurus. They grow up together, they have the same mentors and teachers, but the princes are bitter rivals from their childhood onwards. Lust, greed, honour, betrayal, skill and valour are catalysed by boons, curses, acts of the gods and fate, as the enmity between the cousins hurtles inevitably towards a ghastly fratricidal war that signals the end of the world they have known. On the battlefield of Kuru-kshetra, cousin stands against cousin, student stands against teacher, brother raises arms against brother. Kuru-kshetra has become the metaphorical battlefield of dharma, the symbolic field of righteousness, the arena of both public ethics and personal morality.

Indeed, the *Mahabharata*'s narrative engines are fuelled by karma (the retributive force of one's past actions) and dharma (the elusive principle of righteous conduct). While karma and the supernatural forces that act on the lives of the characters determine what characters can do, dharma puts the individual in a position to choose, to decide for themself what is right and what is wrong. This conflict between determinism and free will lies at the heart of the Hindu epics, and the *Mahabharata* places the problem front and centre – not only in the narrative arcs and actions of its characters, but also in the philosophical discourses that it holds within itself.

The *Mahabharata* contains Hinduism's best-known text, the *Bhagavad Gita*, 'the Song of God', which expounds a radical philosophy of action and being. Krishna, an incarnation of the great god Vishnu, instructs his dear friend and cousin Arjun on how to live in the world and what the significance of his actions will be. The *Gita* is made all the more resonant by the fact that it lifts the central event of the epic, the war, into a metaphor for the moral dilemmas that we face in our everyday lives. On the morning of the battle between the cousins, Arjun, the greatest warrior of his generation, breaks down in front of Krishna, whom he knows only as his human friend, and says that he cannot take up arms against his family, his teachers and his elders, he cannot kill the men with whom he has grown up, the men who made him who he

INTRODUCTION

is. He refuses to fight. Krishna explains that, as a warrior, it is Arjun's dharma, his duty, to fight, and puts forward a doctrine of action that teaches an individual to act always without being attached to the fruit of action. Slowly, through the eighteen chapters of the *Gita*, this manifesto for right action is transformed into a theology of devotion and surrender. Krishna reveals himself to be god, the ultimate reality behind all that we see and do and the refuge of all beings. Arjun is newly empowered to act and blows his mighty conch to signal the commencement of the war.

Here, and in the larger text, the *Mahabharata* relentlessly investigates the questions that lie deepest in the human heart: on what do we base our actions? Do we act for ourselves or for others? What is the individual's place in family and society? Which is our most authentic self? In Hinduism, the principle that underlies all moral action is the doctrine of dharma, a word impossible to translate into any other language, partly because of the vast range of meanings it holds simultaneously and partly because, as the *Mahabharata* itself says, dharma is *sukshma* – it is subtle. Dharma encompasses (but is not restricted to) duty, obligation, responsibility, righteousness, the good, the true, the 'ought' and the 'should', the natural and the constructed laws by which society remains stable and by which the universe is regulated. Karma, which is the other principle of action, affects dharma and vice versa. While karma is about determined choices, dharma is about free will. The interaction of these two forces not only shapes the lives of humans and their relations with those around them but, in the case of Hinduism, also affects what happens to them in their re-births.

Unlike other moral codes – the commandments of the Judaeo-Christian traditions, for example – dharma does not present us with an inviolable template for action, of what we should or should not do. On the contrary, it suggests that these are decisions we need to make for ourselves from the choices that lie before us. Often, we face many right choices (rather than one right and one obviously wrong way to act). These choices are not the same for us all, they depend on who we are and what stage of life we are in, and so dharma is not absolute even though, as a principle, it is eternal. Dharma does not tell us how to be good, it points us in the direction of a far more nuanced and complicated question: what does it mean to be good?

Several incidents in the main story of the *Mahabharata* can be used to think about the ethics we live by and often neglect to question. The *Gita* could prompt us to ask if there is ever such a thing as a righteous war or violence that can be justified, sanctioned even, in the service of a greater good. We can also ask if a system of ethics separate from belief in the existence of a divine being or a set of categorical imperatives can be sustained and be consistent. The catastrophic dice game where Yudhishthir loses everything and then stakes his wife, Draupadi, to win back his kingdom is not only a scene of chilling drama, it also allows us to think about the law (dharma) as an abstraction and its effects on an individual when Draupadi confronts the elders after she has been humiliated in public. The final conversation between Yudhishthir and Duryodhan, his mortal enemy, as the latter lies dying with his legs smashed, will bring up questions about the spoils of war, however justified (or ordained) the war might have been and what the terms of victory and loss truly are. The climax of the story in heaven, where we are confronted with the effects of karma in the afterlife, allows us to think about reconciliation and forgiveness.

Ultimately, the *Mahabharata* is compelling because of its ferociously clear-eyed and unrelenting examination of human nature. It tells stories about people in many different situations:

in solitude, within a family, within society, within a marriage, in love, in hate, in anguish, in exultation. We see people like ourselves in relation to god, we see them search for truth, for knowledge of the self, for tranquility in this life, for freedom from fear, for insights into what lies beyond death. They ask questions about the human condition that we can identify with and understand – the *Mahabharata* entertains these questions and attempts to answer them, not in one way, but in several. The same questions are found in stories told across the world, and each culture and time period provides its own set of answers. The questions are the same everywhere and so, truly, what is in the *Mahabharata* is everywhere and what is not, is nowhere else.

Character List

ABHIMANYU: teenage son of Arjun and Subhadra; brutally killed during the war.

ARJUN: third of the sons of Pandu; born to Pritha; father of Abhimanyu; best friend of Krishna.

ASWA-THAMAN: son of Drona; fights on the side of the Kurus.

BHIMA: strongest of the sons of Pandu; born to Pritha.

BHISHMA: 'grandfather' to the Kurus and the sons of Pandu; fights on the side of the Kurus.

DHRITA-RASHTRA: blind king; father of the one hundred Kuru princes; married to Gandhari.

DRAUPADI: princess of Panchala; wife of Pandu's five sons.

DHRISHTA-DYUMNA: brother of Draupadi; born of a fire sacrifice to kill Drona.

CHARACTER LIST

DRONA: warrior and teacher to the sons of Pandu and the Kuru princes; fights on the side of the Kurus.

DUHSASAN: brother of Duryodhan; humiliates Draupadi.

DURYODHAN: eldest of the Kuru brothers.

GANDHARI: wife of Dhrita-rashtra; mother of the one hundred Kuru princes; wears a blindfold.

KARNA: son of Pritha, brought up by a charioteer; sworn enemy of Arjun and ally of Duryodhan.

KRIPA: martial arts teacher to the sons of Pandu and the Kuru princes.

KRISHNA: incarnation of the great god Vishnu; best friend to Arjun.

MADRI: wife of Pandu; mother of the twins Nakula and Sahadeva.

NAKULA: twin born of Madri.

PANDAV(S): sons of Pandu.

PRITHA: mother of Karna, Yudhishthir, Bhima and Arjun; wife of Pandu.

SAHADEVA: twin born of Madri.

CHARACTER LIST

SAKUNI: brother of Gandhari; expert in dice; ally of the Kurus.

SATYAKI: great warrior; ally of the sons of Pandu.

SALYA: brother of Madri and king of Madra; Karna's charioteer at the end of the war.

SIKHANDIN: born to kill Bhishma.

SISUPALA: enemy of Krishna and the sons of Pandu.

SUBHADRA: wife of Arjun; sister of Krishna; mother of Abhimanyu.

VALADEVA: brother of Krishna.

VIDURA: half-brother of Pandu and Dhritarashtra; elder at the Kuru court.

VIRATA: ruler of the kingdom where the sons of Pandu hide in their last year of exile.

VYASA: narrator of the *Mahabharata* and the biological grandfather of the warring princes.

YUDHISHTHIR: eldest son of Pandu; born to Pritha.

CHARACTER LIST

GODS, CLANS AND PLACES

ADITYAS: minor solar deities.

CHEDI: kingdom ruled by Sisupala.

HASTINA: city of the Kurus, ruled by Dhrita-rashtra.

INDRA-PRASTHA: city built by the sons of Pandu; ruled by Yudhishthir.

MADRA: kingdom ruled by Salya.

MARUTS: storm gods.

MATSYA: kingdom ruled by Virata.

NARAYANA: see VISHNU.

PANCHALA: kingdom ruled by Drupad; natal home of Draupadi.

VISHNU: one of the three great gods of the Hindu pantheon.

VRISHNI: powerful ruling clan.

YADUS/YADAVA: Krishna's clan.

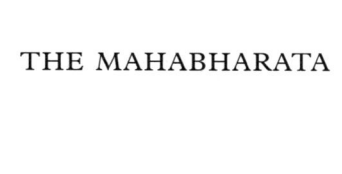

THE EPIC OF THE BHARATAS

BOOK I
ASTRA DARSANA
(*The Tournament*)

The scene of the Epic is the ancient kingdom of the Kurus which flourished along the upper course of the Ganges; and the historical fact on which the Epic is based is a great war which took place between the Kurus and a neighbouring tribe, the Panchalas, in the thirteenth or fourteenth century before Christ.

According to the Epic, Pandu and Dhrita-rashtra, who was born blind, were brothers. Pandu died early, and Dhrita-rashtra became king of the Kurus, and brought up the five sons of Pandu along with his hundred sons.

Yudhishthir, the eldest son of Pandu, was a man of truth and piety; Bhima, the second, was a stalwart fighter; and Arjun, the third son, distinguished himself above all the other princes in arms. The two youngest brothers, Nakula and Sahadeva, were twins. Duryodhan was the eldest son of Dhrita-rashtra and was jealous of his cousins, the sons of Pandu. A tournament was held, and in the course of the day a warrior named Karna, of unknown origin, appeared on the scene and proved himself a worthy rival of Arjun. The rivalry between Arjun and Karna is the leading thought of the Epic, as the rivalry between Achilles and Hector is the leading thought of the Iliad.

It is only necessary to add that the sons of Pandu, as well as Karna, were, like the heroes of Homer, god-born chiefs. Some god inspired the birth of each. Yudhishthir was the son of Dharma or Virtue, Bhima of Vayu or Wind, Arjun of Indra or Rain-god, the twin youngest were the sons of the Aswin twins, and Karna was the son of Surya the Sun, but was believed by himself and by all others to be the son of a simple chariot-driver.

The portion translated in this Book forms Sections cxxxiv. to cxxxvii. of Book i. of the original Epic in Sanscrit (Calcutta edition of 1834).

I
THE GATHERING

Wrathful sons of Dhrita-rashtra, born of Kuru's
   royal race,
Righteous sons of noble Pandu, god-born men of
   godlike grace,

Skill in arms attained these princes from a
   Brahman warrior bold,
Drona, priest and proud preceptor, peerless chief
   of days of old!

Out spake Drona to the monarch in Hastina's
   royal hall,
Spake to Bhishma and to Kripa, spake to lords and
   courtiers all:

"Mark the gallant princes, monarch, trained in
   arms and warlike art,
Let them prove their skill and valour, rein the
   steed and throw the dart."

Answered then the ancient monarch, joyful was his
   royal heart,

"Best of Brahmans and of warriors, nobly hast
  thou done thy part,

Name the place and fix the moment, hold a royal
  tournament,
Publish wide the laws of combat, publish far thy
  king's consent.

Sightless roll these orbs of vision, dark to me is
  noonday light,
Happier men will mark the tourney and the
  peerless princes' fight,

Let the good and wise Vidura serve thy mandate
  and behest,
Let a father's pride and gladness fill this old and
  cheerless breast."

Forthwith went the wise Vidura to his sacred
  duties bound,
Drona, blessed with skill and wisdom, measured
  out the tourney ground,

Clear of jungle was the meadow, by a crystal
  fountain graced,
Drona on the lighted altar holy gifts and offerings
  placed,

ASTRA DARSANA

Holy was the star auspicious, and the hour was
   calm and bright,
Men from distant town and hamlet came to view
   the sacred rite.

Then arose white stately mansions, built by
   architects of fame,
Decked with arms for Kuru's monarch and for
   every royal dame,

And the people built their stages circling round the
   listed green,
And the nobles with their white tents graced the
   fair and festive scene.

Brightly dawned the festal morning, and the
   monarch left his hall,
Bhishma and the pious Kripa with the lords and
   courtiers all,

And they came unto the mansions, gay and
   glittering, gold-encased,
Decked with gems and rich *baidurya*, and with
   strings of pearls be-laced.

Fair Gandhari, queen of Kuru, Pritha, Pandu's
   widowed dame,

Ladies in their gorgeous garments, maids of beauty and of fame,

Mounted on their glittering mansions where the tints harmonious blend,
As, on Meru's golden mountain, queens of heavenly gods ascend!

And the people of the city, Brahmans, Vaisyas, Kshatras bold,
Men from stall and loom and anvil gathered thick, the young and old,

And arose the sound of trumpet and the surging people's cry,
Like the voice of angry ocean, tempest-lashed, sublime and high!

Came the saintly white-robed Drona, white his sacrificial thread,
White his sandal-mark and garlands, white the locks that crowned his head,

With his son renowned for valour walked forth Drona, radiant, high,
So the Moon with Mars conjoinéd walks upon the cloudless sky!

Offerings to the gods immortal then the priestly
 warrior made,
Brahmans with their chanted *mantra* worship and
 obeisance paid,

And the festive note of *sankha* mingled with the
 trumpet's sound,
Throngs of warriors, various-arméd, came unto
 the listed ground.

II
THE PRINCES

Gauntleted and jewel-girdled, now the warlike
 princes came,
With their stately bows and quivers, and their
 swords like wreaths of flame,

Each behind his elder stepping, good Yudhishthir
 first of all,
Each his wondrous skill displaying held the silent
 crowds in thrall.

And the men in admiration marked them with a
 joyful eye,

Or by sudden panic stricken stooped to let the
   arrow fly!

Mounted on their rapid coursers oft the princes
   proved their aim
Racing, hit the targe with arrows lettered with their
   royal name,

With their glinting sunlit weapons shone the
   youths sublime and high,
More than mortals seemed the princes, bright
   Gandharvas of the sky!

Shouts of joy the people uttered as by sudden
   impulse driven,
Mingled voice of tens of thousands struck the
   pealing vault of heaven.

Still the princes shook their weapons, drove the
   deep resounding car,
Or on steed or tusker mounted waged the glorious
   mimic war!

Mighty sword and ample buckler, ponderous mace
   the princes wield,
Brightly gleam their lightning rapiers as they range
   the listed field,

Brave and fearless is their action, and their
    movement quick and light
Skilled and true the thrust and parry of their
    weapons flaming bright!

III

BHIMA AND DURYODHAN

Bhima came and proud Duryodhan with their
    maces lifted high,
Like two cliffs with lofty turrets cleaving through
    the azure sky,

In their warlike arms accoutred with their girded
    loins they stood,
Like two untamed jungle tuskers in the deep and
    echoing wood!

And as tuskers range the forest, so they range the
    spacious field,
Right to left and back they wander and their
    ponderous maces wield.

Unto Kuru's sightless monarch wise Vidura drew
    the scene,

Pritha proudly of the princes spake unto the Kuru queen.

While the stalwart Bhima battled with Duryodhan brave and strong,
Fierce in wrath, for one or other, shouted forth the maddened throng,

"Hail to Kuru prince Duryodhan!" "Hail to Bhima hero proud!"
Sounds like these from surging myriads rose in tumult deep and loud.

And with troubled vision Drona marked the heaving restless plain.
Marked the crowd by anger shaken, like the tempest-shaken main,

To his son he softly whispered quick the tumult to appease,
Part the armed and angry wrestlers, bid the deadly combat cease,

With their lifted clubs the princes slow retired on signal given,
Like the parting of the billows, mighty-heaving, tempest-driven!

Came forth then the ancient Drona on the open battle-ground,
Stopped the drum and lofty trumpet, spake in voice like thunder's sound:

"Bid him come, the gallant Arjun! Pious prince and warrior skilled,
Arjun, born of mighty INDRA, and with VISHNU's prowess filled."

IV
THE ADVENT OF ARJUN

Gauntleted and jewel-girdled, with his bow of ample height,
Archer Arjun pious-hearted to the gods performed a rite,

Then he stepped forth proud and stately in his golden mail encased,
Like the sunlit cloud of evening with the golden rainbow graced,

And a gladness stirred the people all around the listed plain,

Voice of drum and blare of trumpet rose with
   sankha's festive strain!

"Mark! the gallant son of Pandu, whom the happy
   Pritha bore,
Mark! the heir of INDRA'S valour, matchless in his
   arms and lore,

Mark! the warrior young and valiant, peerless in
   his skill of arms,
Mark! the prince of stainless virtue, decked with
   grace and varied charms!"

Pritha heard such grateful voices borne aloft unto
   the sky,
Milk of love suffused her bosom, tear of joy was in
   her eye!

And where rested Kuru's monarch, joyous accents
   struck his ear,
And he turned to wise Vidura seeking for the cause
   to hear:

"Wherefore like the voice of ocean, when the
   tempest winds prevail,
Rise the voices of the people and the spacious skies
   assail?"

ASTRA DARSANA

Answered him the wise Vidura, "It is Pritha's
   gallant boy,
Godlike moves in golden armour, and the people
   shout for joy!"

"Pleased am I," so spake the monarch, "and I bless
   my happy fate,
Pritha's sons like fires of *yajna* sanctify this mighty
   State!"

Now the voices of the people died away and all
   was still,
Arjun to his proud preceptor showed his might
   and matchless skill.

Towering high or lowly bending, on the turf or on
   his car,
With his bow and glist'ning arrows Arjun waged
   the mimic war.

Targets on the wide arena, mighty tough or
   wondrous small,
With his arrows still unfailing, Arjun pierced them
   one and all!

Wild-boar shaped in plates of iron coursed the
   wide-extending field,

In its jaws five glist'ning arrows sent the archer
    wondrous-skilled,

Cow-horn by a thread suspended was by winds
    unceasing swayed,
One and twenty well-aimed arrows on this moving
    mark he laid,

And with equal skill his rapier did the godlike
    Arjun wield,
Whirling round the mace of battle ranged the
    spacious tourney field!

V
THE ADVENT OF KARNA

Now the feats of arms are ended, and the closing
    hour draws nigh,
Music's voice is hushed in silence, and dispersing
    crowds pass by,

Hark! Like welkin-shaking thunder wakes a deep
    and deadly sound,
Clank and din of warlike weapons burst upon the
    tented ground!

ASTRA DARSANA

Are the solid mountains splitting, is it bursting of
 the earth,
Is it tempest's pealing accent whence the lightning
 takes its birth?

Thoughts like these alarm the people for the
 sound is dread and high,
To the gaze of the arena turns the crowd with
 anxious eye!

Gathered round preceptor Drona, Pandu's sons in
 armour bright,
Like the five-starred constellation round the
 radiant Queen of Night,

Gathered round the proud Duryodhan, dreaded
 for his exploits done,
All his brave and warlike brothers and preceptor
 Drona's son,

So the gods encircled INDRA, thunder-wielding,
 fierce and bold,
When he scattered Danu's children in the misty
 days of old!

Pale, before the unknown warrior, gathered
 nations part in twain,

Conqueror of hostile cities, lofty Karna treads the plain,

In his golden mail accoutered and his rings of yellow gold,
Like a moving cliff in stature, arméd comes the chieftain bold,

Pritha, yet unwedded, bore him, peerless archer on the earth,
Portion of the solar radiance, for the Sun inspired his birth!

Like a tusker in his fury, like a lion in his ire,
Like the sun in noontide radiance, like the all-consuming fire,

Lion-like in build and muscle, stately as a golden palm,
Blessed with every manly virtue, peerless, dauntless, proud and calm!

With his looks serene and lofty field of war the chief surveyed,
Scarce to Kripa or to Drona honour and obeisance made,

ASTRA DARSANA

Still the panic-stricken people viewed him with
    unmoving gaze,
Who may be this unknown warrior, questioned
    they in hushed amaze!

Then in voice of pealing thunder spake fair
    Pritha's eldest son
Unto Arjun, Pritha's youngest, each, alas! To each
    unknown:

"All thy feats of weapons, Arjun, done with vain
    and needless boast,
These and greater I accomplish—witness be this
    mighty host!"

Thus spake proud and peerless Karna in his
    accents deep and loud,
And as moved by sudden impulse joyous rose the
    listening crowd,

And a gleam of mighty transport glows in proud
    Duryodhan's heart,
Flames of wrath and jealous anger from the eyes of
    Arjun start,

Drona gave the word, and Karna, Pritha's war-
    beloving son,

With his sword and with his arrows did the feats
  by Arjun done!

VI
THE RIVAL WARRIORS

Joyful was the proud Duryodhan, gladness
  gleamed upon his face,
And he spake to gallant Karna with a loving fond
  embrace:

"Welcome, mighty arméd chieftain! thou hast
  victor's honours won,
Thine is all my wealth and kingdom, name thy
  wish and it is done!"

Answered Karna to Duryodhan, "Prince! thy word
  is good as deed,
But I seek to combat Arjun and to win the victor's
  meed,"

"Noble is the boon thou seekest," answered Kuru's
  prince of fame,
"Be a joy unto your comrades, let the foeman
  dread thy name!"

ASTRA DARSANA

Anger flamed in Arjun's bosom, and he spake in accents rude
Unto Karna who in triumph calm and proud and fearless stood:

"Chief! Who comest uninvited, pratest in thy lying boast,
Thou shalt die the death of braggarts—witness be this mighty host!"

Karna answered calm and proudly, "Free this listed field to all,
Warriors enter by their prowess, wait not, Arjun, for thy call,

Warlike chieftains take their places by their strength of arm and might,
And their warrant is their falchion, valour sanctifies their right,

Angry word is coward's weapon, Arjun, speak with arrows keen,
Till I lay thee, witness Drona, low upon the listed green!"

Drona gave the word impartial, wrathful Arjun, dread of foes,

Parted from his loving brothers, in his glist'ning
    arms arose,

Karna clasped the Kuru's princes, parted from
    them one and all,
With his bow and ample quiver proudly stepped
    the warrior tall.

Now the clouds with lurid flashes gathered
    darkling, thick and high,
Lines of cranes like gleams of laughter sailed
    across the gloomy sky,

Rain-god INDRA over Arjun watched with father's
    partial love,
Sun-god SURYA over Karna shed his light from far
    above,

Arjun stood in darkening shadow by the inky
    clouds concealed,
Bold and bright in open sunshine radiant Karna
    stood revealed!

Proud Duryodhan and his brothers stood by
    Karna calm and bold,
Drona stood by gallant Arjun, and brave Bhishma
    warrior old,

Women too with partial glances viewed the one or other chief,
But by equal love divided silent Pritha swooned in grief!

Wise Vidura, true to duty, with an anxious hurry came,
Sandal-drops and sprinkled waters roused the woe-distracted dame,

And she saw her sons in combat, words of woe she uttered none,
Speechless wept, for none must fathom Karna was her eldest son!

VII

THE ANOINTMENT OF KARNA

Crested Karna, helméd Arjun, proudly trod the spacious green,
Kripa, skilled in herald's duties, spake upon the dreadful scene:

"This is helmet-wearing Arjun, sprung of Kuru's mighty race,

*Pandu's son and borne by Pritha, prince of worth and
   warlike grace,*

*Long-armed Chief! declare thy lineage, and the race
   thou dost adorn,*
*Name thy mother and thy father, and the house that
   saw thee born,*

*By the rules of war Prince Arjun claims his rival chief
   to know,*
*Princes may not draw their weapon 'gainst a base and
   nameless foe!"*

Karna silent heard this mandate, rank nor lineage
   could he claim,
Like a raindrop-pelted lotus bent his humble head
   in shame!

"Prince we reckon," cried Duryodhan, "not the
   man of birth alone,
Warlike leader of his forces as a prince and chief
   we own,

Karna by his warlike valour is of crownéd kings
   the peer,
Karna shall be crownéd monarch, nations shall his
   mandate hear!"

ASTRA DARSANA

Forth they brought the corn and treasure, golden coin and water jar,
On the throne they seated Karna famed in many a deathful war,

Brahmans chanted sacred *mantra* which the holy books ordain,
And anointed crownéd Karna king of Anga's fair domain,

And they raised the red umbrella, and they waved the *chowri* fan,
"Blessings on the crownéd monarch! honour to the bravest man!"

Now the holy rites accomplished, in his kingly robes arrayed
Karna unto prince Duryodhan thus in grateful accents prayed:

"Gift of kingdom, good Duryodhan, speaketh well thy noble heart,
What return can grateful Karna humbly render on his part?"

"Grant thy friendship," cried Duryodhan, "for no other boon I crave,

Be Duryodhan's dearest comrade, be his helper
 true and brave,"

"Be it so!" responded Karna, with a proud and
 noble grace,
And he sealed his loyal friendship in a loving fond
 embrace!

VIII

THE CHARIOT-DRIVER

Dewed with drops of toil and languor, lo! a
 chariot-driver came,
Loosely hung his scanty garments, and a staff
 upheld his frame,

Karna, now a crownéd monarch, to the humble
 Suta sped,
As a son unto a father, reverently bent his head!

With his scanty cloth the driver sought his dusty
 feet to hide,
And he hailed him as a father hails his offspring in
 his pride,

ASTRA DARSANA

And he clasped unto his bosom crownéd Karna's
  noble head,
And on Karna's dripping forehead, fresh and
  loving tear-drops shed!

Is he son of chariot-driver? Doubts arose in
  Bhima's mind,
And he sought to humble Karna with reproachful
  words unkind:

"Wilt thou, high-descended hero, with a Kuru
  cross thy brand?
But the goad of cattle-drivers better suits, my
  friend, thy hand!

Wilt thou as a crownéd monarch rule a mighty
  nation's weal?
As the jackals of the jungle sacrificial offerings
  steal!"

Quivered Karna's lips in anger, word of answer
  spake he none,
But a deep sigh shook his bosom, and he gazed
  upon the sun!

THE MAHABHARATA

IX
CLOSE OF THE DAY

Like a lordly tusker rising from a beauteous
    lotus lake,
Rose Duryodhan from his brothers, proudly thus
    to Bhima spake:

"With such insults seek not, Bhima, thus to cause
    a warrior grief,
Bitter taunts but ill befit thee, warlike tiger-waisted
    chief,

Proudest chief may fight the humblest, for like
    river's noble course,
Noble deeds proclaim the warrior, and we
    question not their source!

Teacher Drona, priest and warrior, owns a poor
    and humble birth,
Kripa, noblest of Gautamas, springeth from the
    lowly earth,

Known to me thy lineage Bhima, thine and of thy
    brothers four,

ASTRA DARSANA

Amorous gods your birth imparted, so they say, in
    days of yore!

Mark the great and gallant Karna decked in rings
    and weapons fair
She-deer breeds not lordly tigers in her poor and
    lowly lair,

Karna comes to rule the wide earth, not fair
    Anga's realms alone,
By his valour and his virtue, by the homage which
    I own,

And if prince or arméd chieftain doth my word or
    deed gainsay,
Let him take his bow and quiver, meet me in a
    deadly fray!"

Loud applauses greet the challenge and the
    people's joyful cry,
But the thickening shades of darkness fill the earth
    and evening sky

And the red lamp's fitful lustre shone upon the
    field around,
Slowly with the peerless Karna proud Duryodhan
    left the ground.

Pandu's sons with warlike Drona marked the
   darksome close of day
And with Kripa and with Bhishma homeward
   silent bent their way

"Arjun is the gallant victor!" "Valiant Karna's won
   the day!"
"Prince Duryodhan is the winner!" Various thus
   the people say

By some secret sign appriséd Pritha knew her
   gallant boy,
Saw him crownéd king of Anga with a mother's
   secret joy,

And with greater joy Duryodhan fastened Karna
   to his side,
Feared no longer Arjun's prowess, Arjun's skill of
   arms and pride

E'en Yudhishthir reckoned Karna mightiest
   warrior on the earth,
Half misdoubted Arjun's prowess, Arjun's skill and
   warlike worth!

Book II
Swayamvara
(*The Bride's Choice*)

The mutual jealousies of the princes increased from day to day, and when Yudhishthir, the eldest of all the princes and the eldest son of the late Pandu, was recognised heir-apparent, the anger of Duryodhan and his brothers knew no bounds. And they formed a dark scheme to kill the sons of Pandu.

The sons of Pandu were induced with their mother to pay a visit to a distant town called Varanavata. A house had been built there for their residence, constructed of inflammable materials. At the appointed time fire was set to the house; but the five brothers and their mother escaped the conflagration through a subterranean passage, retired into forests, and lived in the disguise of Brahmans.

In course of time they heard of the approaching celebrations of the marriage of the princess of Panchala, an ancient kingdom in the vicinity of modern Kanouj. All the monarchs of Northern India were invited, and the bride would choose her husband from among the assembled kings according to the ancient *Swayamvara* custom. The five sons of Pandu decided to go and witness the ceremony.

The portion translated in this Book formed Sections clxxxiv. to cxxxix. of Book i. of the original text.

I
JOURNEY TO PANCHALA

Now the righteous sons of Pandu, wand'ring far
    from day to day,
Unto South Panchala's country glad and joyful
    held their way,

For when travelling with their mother, so it
    chanced by will of fate,
They were met by pious Brahmans bound for
    South Panchala's State,

And the pure and holy Brahmans hailed the youth
    of noble fame,
Asked them whither they would journey, from
    what distant land they came,

"From the land of Ekachakra," good Yudhishthir
    answered so,
"With our ancient mother travelling unto distant
    lands we go."

"Heard ye not," the Brahmans questioned, "in
    Panchala's fair domain,

Drupad, good and gracious monarch, doth a
    mighty feast ordain,

To that festive land we journey, Drupad's
    bounteous gifts to share,
And to see the *swayamvara* of Panchala's princess
    fair,—

Human mother never bore her, human bosom
    never fed,
From the Altar sprang the maiden who some noble
    prince will wed!

Soft her eyes like lotus-petal, sweet her tender
    jasmine form,
And a maiden's stainless honour doth her gentle
    soul inform,

And her brother, mailed and arméd with his bow
    and arrows dire,
Radiant as the blazing altar, sprang from
    Sacrificial Fire!

Fair the sister slender-waisted, dowered with
    beauty rich and rare,
And like fragrance of blue lotus, perfumes all the
    sweetened air,

SWAYAMVARA

She will choose from noble suitors gathered from
 the west and east,
Bright and fair shall be the wedding, rich and
 bounteous be the feast!

Kings will come from distant regions sacrificing
 wealth and gold,
Stainless monarchs versed in *sastra*, pious-hearted,
 mighty-souled,

Handsome youths and noble princes from each
 near and distant land,
Car-borne chieftains bold and skilful, brave of
 heart and stout of hand!

And to win the peerless princess they will scatter
 presents rare,
Food and milch-kine, wealth and jewels, gold and
 gifts and garments fair,

Noble gifts we take as Brahmans, bless the rite
 with gladsome heart,
Share the feast so rich and bounteous, then with
 joyful minds depart.

Actors, mimes, and tuneful minstrels fair
 Panchala's court will throng,

Famed reciters of *puranas*, dancers skilled and
   wrestlers strong,

Come with us, the wedding witness, share the
   banquet rich and rare,
Pleased with gifts and noble presents to your
   distant home repair.

Dowered ye are with princely beauty, like the
   radiant gods above,
Even on you the partial princess may surrender
   heart and love,

And this youth so tall and stalwart, mighty-arméd,
   strong and bold,
He may win in feats of valour rich renown and
   wealth untold!"

"Be it so," Yudhishthir answered, "to Panchala we
   repair,
View the wedding of the princess and the royal
   bounty share,"

And the righteous sons of Pandu with the
   Brahmans took their way,
Where in South Panchala's kingdom mighty
   Drupad held his sway,

SWAYAMVARA

Now it fell, the saintly *rishi*, deathless bard of
 deathless lay,
Herald of the holy *Vedas*, Vyasa stood before
 their way.

And the princes bowed unto him and received his
 blessings kind,
By his mandate to Panchala went with pleased and
 joyful mind!

Jungle woods and silver waters round their sylvan
 pathway lay,
Halting at each wayside station marched the
 princes day by day,

Stainless and intent on *sastra*, fair in speech and
 pure in heart,
Travelling slow they reached Panchala, saw its
 spacious town and mart,

Saw the fort, bazaar and city, saw the spire and
 shining dome,
In a potter's distant cottage made their humble
 unknown home,

And disguised as pious Brahmans sons of Pandu
 begged their food,

People knew not Kuru's princes in that dwelling
   poor and rude.

II
THE WEDDING ASSEMBLY

To the helméd son of Pandu, Arjun pride of
   Kuru's race,
Drupad longed to give his daughter peerless in her
   maiden grace,

And of massive wood unbending, Drupad made a
   stubborn bow,
Saving Arjun prince or chieftain might not bend
   the weapon low,

And he made a whirling discus, hung it 'neath the
   open sky,
And beyond the whirling discus placed a target far
   and high,

"Whoso strings this bow," said Drupad, "hits the
   target in his pride
Through the high and circling discus, wins
   Panchala's princely bride!"

SWAYAMVARA

And they spake the monarch's mandate in the
    kingdoms near and far,
And from every town and country princes came
    and chiefs of war,

Came the pure and saintly *rishis* for to bless the
    holy rite,
Came the Kurus with brave Karna in their pride
    and matchless might,

Brahmans came from distant regions with their
    sacred learning blest,
Drupad with a royal welcome greeted every
    honoured guest.

Now the festal day approacheth! Gathering men
    with ocean's voice,
Filled the wide and circling stages to behold the
    maiden's choice,

Royal guests and princely suitors came in pomp of
    wealth and pride,
Car-borne chiefs and mailéd warriors came to win
    the beauteous bride!

North-east of the festive city they enclosed a level
    ground,

Towering dome and stately palace cunning
    builders built around,

And by moat and wall surrounded, pierced by gate
    and archéd door,
By a canopy of splendour was the red field
    covered o'er!

Now the festal day approacheth! Sacred censers
    fragrance lent,
Sprinkled *chandan* spread its coolness, wreaths
    were hung of sweetest scent,

All around were swan-white mansions, lofty domes
    and turrets high,
Like the peaks of white Kailasa cleaving through
    the azure sky!

Sparkling gems the chambers lighted, golden nets
    the windows laced,
Spacious stairs so wide and lofty were with
    beauteous carpets graced,

Rich festoons and graceful garlands gently waved
    like streamers gay,
And the swan-like silver mansions glinted in the
    light of day!

SWAYAMVARA

Now the festal day approacheth! High the royal
    chambers lay,
With their lofty gilded turrets like the peaks of
    Himalay,

In these halls in pride and splendour dwelt each
    rich and royal guest,
Fired by mutual emulation, and in costly jewels
    drest,

Decked and perfumed sat these rulers, mighty-
    arméd, rich in fame,
Lion-monarchs, noble-destined, chiefs of pure and
    spotless name,

Pious to the mighty BRAHMA, and their subjects'
    hope and stay,
Loved of all for noble actions, kind and virtuous in
    their sway.

Now the festal day approacheth! like the heaving
    of the main,
Surge the ranks of gathered nations o'er the wide
    and spacious plain,

Pandu's sons in guise of Brahmans mix with
    Brahmans versed in lore,

Mark proud Drupad's wealth and splendour,
    gazing, wondering evermore,

Dancers charm the gathered people, singers sing
    and actors play,
Fifteen days of festive splendour greet the
    concourse rich and gay.

III
THE BRIDE

Sound the drum and voice the *sankha*! Brightly
    dawns the bridal day,
Fresh from morning's pure ablutions comes the
    bride in garments gay,

And her golden bridal garland, carrying on her
    graceful arm,
Softly, sweetly, steps Draupadi, queen of every
    winning charm!

Then a Brahman versed in *mantra*, ancient priest
    of lunar race,
Lights the Fire, with pious offerings seek its
    blessings and its grace,

SWAYAMVARA

Whispered words of benediction saints and holy
    men repeat,
Conch and trumpet's voice is silent, hushed the
    lofty war-drum's beat,

And there reigns a solemn silence, and in stately
    pomp and pride,
Drupad's son leads forth his sister, fair Panchala's
    beauteous bride!

In his loud and lofty accents like the distant
    thunder's sound,
Drupad's son his father's wishes thus proclaims to
    all around:

*"Mark this bow, assembled monarchs, and the target
    hung on high,
Through yon whirling piercéd discus let five glist' ning
    arrows fly,*

*Whoso, born of noble lineage, hits the far
    suspended aim,
Let him stand and as his guerdon Drupad's beauteous
    maiden claim!"*

Then he turns unto Draupadi, tells each prince
    and suitor's name,

Tells his race and lofty lineage, and his warlike
  deeds of fame.

IV
THE SUITORS

"Brave Duryodhan and his brothers, princes of the
  Kuruland,
Karna proud and peerless archer, sister! seek thy
  noble hand,

And Gandhara's warlike princes, Bhoja's monarch
  true and bold,
And the son of mighty Drona, all bedecked in
  gems and gold!

King and prince from Matsya kingdom grace this
  noble wedding-feast,
Monarchs from more distant regions north and
  south and west and east,

Tamralipta and Kalinga on the eastern
  ocean wave,
Pattan's port whose hardy children western
  ocean's dangers brave!

SWAYAMVARA

From the distant land of Madra car-borne
    monarch Salya came,
And from Dwarka's sea-girt regions Valadeva
    known to fame,

Valadeva and his brother Krishna sprung from
    Yadu's race,
Of the Vrishni clan descended, soul of truth and
    righteous grace!

This is mighty Jayadratha come from Sindhu's
    sounding shore,
Famed for warlike feats of valour, famed alike for
    sacred lore,

This is fair Kosala's monarch whose bright deeds
    our heralds sing,
From the sturdy soil of Chedi, this is Chedi's
    peerless king!

This is mighty Jarasandha, come from far
    Magadha's land,
These are other princely suitors, sister! eager for
    thy hand,

All the wide earth's warlike rulers seek to shoot the
    distant aim,

Princess, whoso hits the target, choose as thine
  that prince of fame!"

Decked with jewels, young and valiant, all aflame
  with soft desire,
Conscious of their worth and valour, all the suitors
  rose in ire,

Nobly born, of lofty presence, full of young
  unyielding pride,
Like the tuskers wild and lordly on Himalay's
  wooded side!

Each his rival marks as foeman as in field of deadly
  strife,
Each regards the fair Draupadi as his own his
  queenly wife,

On the gorgeous field they gather by a maddening
  passion fired,
And they strive as strove the bright gods, when by
  Uma's love inspired!

And the gods in cloud-borne chariots came to
  view the scene so fair,
Bright ADITYAS in their splendour, MARUTS in the
  moving air,

SWAYAMVARA

Winged *Suparnas*, scaly *Nagas*, saints celestial pure
   and high,
For their music famed, *Gandharvas*, fair *Apsaras* of
   the sky!

Valadeva armed with ploughshare, Krishna chief
   of righteous fame,
With the other Yadu chieftains to that wondrous
   bridal came,

Krishna marked the sons of Pandu eager for the
   maiden queen,
Like wild tuskers for a lotus, like the fire that lurks
   unseen,

And he knew the warlike brothers in their holy
   Brahman guise,
Pointed them to Valadeva, gazing with a glad
   surprise!

But the other chiefs and monarchs with their eyes
   upon the bride,
Marked nor knew the sons of Pandu sitting
   speechless by their side,

And the long-armed sons of Pandu smitten by
   KANDARPA'S dart,

Looked on her with longing languor and with love-
    impassioned heart!

Bright Immortals gaily crowding viewed the scene
    surpassing fair,
Heavenly blossoms soft descending with a perfume
    filled the air,

Bright celestial cars in concourse sailed upon the
    cloudless sky,
Drum and flute and harp and tabor sounded deep
    and sounded high!

V
TRIAL OF SKILL

Uprose one by one the suitors, marking still the
    distant aim,
Mighty monarchs, gallant princes, chiefs of proud
    and warlike fame,

Decked in golden crown and necklace, and
    inflamed by pride and love,
Stoutly strove the eager suitors viewing well the
    targe above,

SWAYAMVARA

Strove to string the weapon vainly, tough
 unbending was the bow,
Slightly bent, rebounding quickly, laid the gallant
 princes low!

Strove the handsome suitors vainly, decked in gem
 and burnished gold,
Reft of diadem and necklace, fell each chief and
 warrior bold,

Reft of golden crown and garland, shamed and
 humbled in their pride,
Groaned the suitors in their anguish, sought no
 more Panchala's bride!

Uprose Karna, peerless archer, proudest of the
 archers he,
And he went and strung the weapon, fixed the
 arrows gallantly,

Stood like SURYA in his splendour and like AGNI
 in his flame,—
Pandu's sons in terror whispered, Karna sure must
 hit the aim!

But in proud and queenly accents Drupad's
 queenly daughter said:

"Monarch's daughter, born a Kshatra, Suta's son I
  will not wed,"

Karna heard with crimsoned forehead, left the
  emprise almost done,
Left the bow already circled, silent gazed upon
  the Sun!

Uprose Chedi's haughty monarch, mightiest of the
  monarchs he,
Other kings had failed inglorious, Sisupala stood
  forth free,

Firm in heart and fixed in purpose, bent the tough
  unbending bow,
Vainly! for the bow rebounding laid the haughty
  monarch low!

Uprose sturdy Jarasandha, far Magadha's mighty
  chief,
Held the bow and stood undaunted, tall and
  stately as a cliff,

But once more the bow rebounded, fell the
  monarch in his shame,
Left in haste Panchala's mansions for the region
  whence he came!

SWAYAMVARA

Uprose Salya, king of Madra, with his wondrous
    skill and might,
Faltering, on his knees descending, fell in sad
    inglorious plight,

Thus each monarch fell and faltered, merry
    whispers went around,
And the sound of stifled laughter circled round the
    festive ground!

VI
THE DISGUISED ARJUN

Hushed the merry sound of laughter, hushed each
    suitor in his shame,
Arjun, godlike son of Pritha, from the ranks of
    Brahmans came,

Guised as priest serene and holy, fair as INDRA'S
    rainbow bright,
All the Brahmans shook their deerskins, cheered
    him in their hearts' delight!

Some there were with sad misgivings heard the
    sound of joyous cheer

And their minds were strangely anxious, whispered
   murmurs spake their fear:

"Wondrous bow which Sisupala, mighty Salya
   could not strain,
Jarasandha famed for prowess strove to bend the
   string in vain,

Can a Brahman weak by nature, and in warlike
   arms untrained,
Wield the bow which crownéd monarchs, long-
   armed chieftains have not strained?

Sure the Brahman boy in folly dares a foolish
   thoughtless deed,
And amidst this throng of monarchs shame will be
   our only meed,

Youth in youthful pride or madness will a foolish
   emprise dare,
Sager men should stop his rashness and the
   Brahman's honour spare!"

"Shame he will not bring unto us," other
   Brahmans made reply,
"Rather, in this throng of monarchs, rich renown
   and honour high,

SWAYAMVARA

Like a tusker strong and stately, like Himalay's
    towering crest,
Stands unmoved the youthful Brahman, ample-
    shouldered, deep in chest,

Lion-like his gait is agile, and determined is his air,
Trust me he can do an emprise who hath lofty will
    to dare!

He will do the feat of valour, will not bring
    disgrace and stain,
Nor is task in all this wide earth which a Brahman
    tries in vain,

Holy men subsist on wild fruits, in the strength of
    penance strong,
Spare in form, in spirit mightier than the mightiest
    warlike throng!

Ask not if 'tis right or foolish when a Brahman
    tries his fate,
If it leads to woe or glory, fatal fall or fortune
    great,

Son of *rishi* Jamadagni baffled kings and chieftains
    high,

And Agastya stainless *rishi* drained the boundless
 ocean dry,

Let this young and daring Brahman undertake the
 warlike deed,
Let him try and by his prowess win the victor's
 noble meed!"

While the Brahmans deep revolving hopes and
 timid fears expressed,
By the bow the youthful Arjun stood unmoved like
 mountain crest,

Silent round the wondrous weapon thrice the
 mighty warrior went,
To the God of Gods, ISANA, in a silent prayer
 he bent,

Then the bow which gathered warriors vainly tried
 to bend and strain,
And the monarchs of the wide earth sought to
 string and wield in vain,

Godlike Arjun born of INDRA, filled with VISHNU'S
 matchless might,
Bent the wondrous bow of Drupad, fixed the
 shining darts aright,

SWAYAMVARA

Through the disc the shining arrows fly with
    strange and hissing sound,
Hit and pierce the distant target, bring it
    thundering on the ground!

Shouts of joy and loud applauses did the mighty
    feat declare,
Heavenly blossoms soft descended, heavenly
    music thrilled the air,

And the Brahmans shook their deerskins, but each
    irritated chief
In a lowly muttered whisper spake his rising rage
    and grief,

Sankha's note and voice of trumpet Arjun's
    glorious deed prolong,
Bards and heralds chant his praises in a proud and
    deathless song!

Drupad in the Brahman's mantle knew the hero
    proud and brave,
'Gainst the rage of baffled suitors sought the
    gallant prince to save,

With his twin-born youngest brothers left
    Yudhishthir, peaceful, good,

Bhima marked the gathering tempest and by
    gallant Arjun stood!

Like a queen the beauteous maiden smiled upon
    the archer brave,
Flung on him the bridal garland and the bridal
    robe she gave,

Arjun by his skill and prowess won Panchala's
    princess-bride,
People's shouts and Brahmans' blessings sounded
    joyful far and wide!

VII
THE TUMULT

Spake the suitors, anger-shaken, like a forest
    tempest-torn,
As Panchala's courteous monarch came to greet a
    Brahman-born:

"Shall he like the grass of jungle trample us in
    haughty pride,
To a prating priest and Brahman wed the proud
    and peerless bride?

SWAYAMVARA

To our hopes like nourished saplings shall he now
 the fruit deny,
Monarch proud who insults monarchs sure a
 traitor's death shall die,

Honour for his rank we know not, have no mercy
 for his age,
Perish foe of crownéd monarchs, victim to our
 righteous rage!

Hath he asked us to his palace, favoured us with
 royal grace,
Feasted us with princely bounty, but to compass
 our disgrace,

In this concourse of great monarchs, glorious like
 a heavenly band,
Doth he find no likely suitor for his beauteous
 daughter's hand?

And this rite of *swayamvara*, so our sacred laws
 ordain,
Is for warlike Kshatras only, priests that custom
 shall not stain,

If this maiden on a Brahman casts her eye, devoid
 of shame,

THE MAHABHARATA

Let her expiate her folly in a pyre of blazing
  flame!

Leave the priestling in his folly sinning through a
  Brahman's greed,
For we wage no war with Brahmans and forgive a
  foolish deed,

Much we owe to holy Brahmans for our realm and
  wealth and life,
Blood of priest or wise preceptor shall not stain
  our noble strife,

In the blood of sinful Drupad we the righteous
  laws maintain,
Such disgrace in future ages monarchs shall not
  meet again!"

Spake the suitors, tiger-hearted, iron-handed, bold
  and strong,
Fiercely bent on blood and vengeance blindly rose
  the maddened throng,

On they came, the angry monarchs, armed for
  cruel vengeful strife,
Drupad midst the holy Brahmans trembling fled
  for fear of life,

SWAYAMVARA

Like wild elephants of jungle rushed the kings
　　upon their foes,
Calm and stately, stalwart Bhima and the gallant
　　Arjun rose!

With a wilder rage the monarchs viewed these
　　brothers cross their path,
Rushed upon the daring warriors for to slay them
　　in their wrath,

Weaponless was noble Bhima, but in strength like
　　lightning's brand,
Tore a tree with peerless prowess, shook it as a
　　mighty wand!

And the foe-compelling warrior held that mace of
　　living wood,
Strong as death with deadly weapon, facing all his
　　foes he stood,

Arjun too with godlike valour stood unmoved, his
　　bow in hand,
Side by side the dauntless brothers faced the fierce
　　and fiery band!

VIII
KRISHNA TO THE RESCUE

Krishna knew the sons of Pandu though in robes
    of Brahmans dressed,
To his elder, Valadeva, thus his inner thoughts
    expressed:

"Mark that youth with bow and arrow and with
    lion's lordly gait,
He is helmet-wearing Arjun! greatest warrior
    midst the great,

Mark his mate, with tree uprooted how he meets
    the suitor band,
Save the tiger-waisted Bhima none can claim such
    strength of hand!

And the youth with eyes like lotus, he who left the
    court erewhile,
He is pious-souled Yudhishthir, man without a sin
    or guile,

And the others by Yudhishthir, Pandu's twin-born
    sons are they,

With these sons the righteous Pritha 'scaped where
    death and danger lay,

For the jealous, fierce Duryodhan darkly schemed
    their death by fire,
But the righteous sons of Pandu 'scaped his
    unrelenting ire!"

Krishna rose amidst the monarchs, strove the
    tumult to appease,
And unto the angry suitors spake in words of
    righteous peace,

Monarchs bowed to Krishna's mandate, left
    Panchala's festive land,
Arjun took the beauteous princess, gently led her
    by the hand.

Book III
Rajasuya
(*The Imperial Sacrifice*)

A curious incident followed the bridal of Draupadi. The five sons of Pandu returned with her to the potter's house, where they were living on alms according to the custom of Brahmans, and the brothers reported to their mother that they had received a great gift on that day. "Enjoy ye the gift in common," replied their mother, not knowing what it was. And as a mother's mandate cannot be disregarded, Draupadi became the common wife of the five brothers.

The real significance of this strange legend is unknown. The custom of brothers marrying a common wife prevails to this day in Thibet and among the hill-tribes of the Himalayas, but it never prevailed among the Aryan Hindus of India. It is distinctly prohibited in their laws and institutes, and finds no sanction in their literature, ancient or modern. The legend in the *Maha-bharata*, of brothers marrying a wife in common, stands alone and without a parallel in Hindu traditions and literature.

Judging from the main incidents of the Epic, Draupadi might rather be regarded as the wife of the eldest brother Yudhishthir. Bhima had already mated himself to a female in a forest, by whom he had a son, Ghatotkacha, who distinguished himself in war later on. Arjun too married the sister of Krishna, shortly after Draupadi's bridal, and had by her a son, Abhimanyu, who was one of the heroes of the war. On the other hand, Yudhishthir took to himself no wife save Draupadi, and she was crowned with Yudhishthir in the Rajasuya or Imperial Sacrifice. Notwithstanding the legend, therefore, Draupadi might be regarded as wedded to Yudhishthir, though won by the skill of Arjun, and this assumption would be in keeping with Hindu customs and laws, ancient and modern.

The jealous Duryodhan heard that his contrivance to kill his cousins at Varanavata had failed. He also heard that they had found a powerful friend in Drupad, and had formed an alliance with him. It was no longer possible to keep them from their rightful inheritance. The Kuru kingdom was accordingly parcelled; Duryodhan retained the eastern and richer portion with its ancient capital *Hastina-pura* on the Ganges; and the sons of Pandu were given the western portion on the Jumna, which was then a forest and a wilderness.

RAJASUYA

The sons of Pandu cleared the forest and built a new capital *Indra-prastha,* the supposed ruins of which, near modern Delhi, are still pointed out to the curious traveller.

Yudhishthir, the eldest of the five sons of Pandu, and now king of Indra-prastha, resolved to perform the Rajasuya sacrifice, which was a formal assumption of the Imperial title over all the kings of ancient India. His brothers went out with troops in all directions to proclaim his supremacy over all surrounding kings. Jarasandha, the powerful and semi-civilised king of Magadha or South Behar, opposed and was killed; but other monarchs recognised the supremacy of Yudhishthir and came to the sacrifice with tributes. King Dhrita-rashtra and his sons, now reigning at Hastina-pura, were politely invited to take a share in the performance of the sacrifice.

The portion translated in this Book forms Sections xxxiii. to xxxvi. and Section xliv. of Book ii. of the original.

I
THE ASSEMBLAGE OF KINGS

Ancient halls of proud Hastina mirrored bright on
 Ganga's wave!
Thither came the son of Pandu, young Nakula
 true and brave,

Came to ask Hastina's monarch, chief of Kuru's
 royal race,
To partake Yudhishthir's banquet and his sacrifice
 to grace.

Dhrita-rashtra came in gladness unto Indra-
 prastha's town,
Marked its new-built tower and turret on the azure
 Jumna frown,

With him came preceptor Kripa, and the ancient
 Bhishma came,
Elders of the race of Kuru, chiefs and Brahmans
 known to fame.

Monarchs came from distant regions to partake
 the holy rite,

RAJASUYA

Warlike chiefs from court and castle in their arms
    accoutred bright,

Kshatras came with ample tribute for the holy
    sacrifice,
Precious gems and costly jewels, gold and gifts of
    untold price.

Proud Duryodhan and his brothers came in fair
    and friendly guise,
With the ancient Kuru monarch and Vidura good
    and wise,

With his son came brave Suvala from Gandhara's
    distant land,
Car-borne Salya, peerless Karna, came with bow
    and spear and brand.

Came the priest and proud preceptor Drona
    skilled in arms and lore,
Jayadratha famed for valour came from Sindhu's
    sounding shore,

Drupad came with gallant princes from Panchala's
    land of fame,
Salwa lord of outer nations to the mighty
    gathering came.

Bhagadatta came in chariot from the land of
   nations brave,
Prag-jyotisha, where the red sun wakes on
   Brahma-putra's wave,

With him came untutored *Mlechchas* who beside
   the ocean dwell,
Uncouth chiefs of dusky nations from the lands
   where mountains swell.

Came Virata, Matsya's monarch, and his warlike
   sons and bold,
Sisupala, king of Chedi, with his son bedecked
   in gold.

Came the warlike chiefs of Vrishni from the shores
   of Western Sea,
And the lords of Madhya-desa, ever warlike
   ever free!

II
FEAST AND SACRIFICE

Jumna's dark and limpid waters laved Yudhishthir's
   palace walls

RAJASUYA

And to hail him *Dharma-raja*, monarchs thronged
   his royal halls,

He to honoured kings and chieftains with a royal
   grace assigned
Palaces with sparkling waters and with trees
   umbrageous lined,

Honoured thus, the mighty monarchs lived in
   mansions milky white,
Like the peaks of famed Kailasa lifting proud their
   snowy height!

Graceful walls that swept the meadows circled
   round the royal halls,
Nets of gold belaced the casements, gems
   bedecked the shining walls,

Flights of steps led up to chambers
   many-tinted-carpet-graced,
And festooning fragrant garlands were harmonious
   interlaced!

Far below from spacious gateways rose the
   people's gathering cry,
And from far the swan-white mansions caught the
   ravished gazer's eye,

Richly graced with precious metals shone the
    turrets bright and gay,
Like the rich-ored shining turrets of the lofty
    Himalay,

And the scene bedecked by *rishis* and by priests
    and kings of might,
Shone like azure sky in splendour graced by
    deathless Sons of Light!

Spake Yudhishthir unto Bhishma, elder of the
    Kuru race,
Unto Drona proud preceptor, rich in lore and
    warlike grace,

Spake to wise preceptor Kripa, versed in sacred
    rites of old,
To Duryodhan and his brothers, honoured guests
    and kinsmen bold:

"Friends and kinsmen, grant your favour and your
    sweet affection lend,
May your kindness ever helpful poor Yudhishthir's
    rite attend,

As your own, command my treasure, costly gifts
    and wealth untold,

RAJASUYA

To the poor and to the worthy scatter free my
  gems and gold!"

Speaking thus he made his *diksha*, and to holy
  work inclined,
To his friends and to his kinsmen all their various
  tasks assigned:

Proud Duhsasan in his bounty spread the rich and
  sumptuous feast,
Drona's son with due devotion greeted saint and
  holy priest,

Sanjay with a regal honour welcomed king and
  chief of might,
Bhishma and the pious Drona watched the
  sacrificial rite,

Kripa guarded wealth and treasure, gold and gems
  of untold price,
And with presents unto Brahmans sanctified the
  sacrifice,

Dhrita-rashtra, old and sightless, through the
  scene of gladness strayed,
With a careful hand Vidura all the mighty cost
  defrayed,

THE MAHABHARATA

Proud Duryodhan took the tribute which the
    chiefs and monarchs paid,
Pious Krishna unto Brahmans honour and
    obeisance made.

'Twas a gathering fair and wondrous on fair
    Jumna's sacred shore,
Tributes in a thousand *nishkas* every willing
    monarch bore,

Costly gifts proclaimed the homage of each prince
    of warlike might,
Chieftains vied with rival chieftains to assist the
    holy rite.

Bright Immortals, robed in sunlight, sailed across
    the liquid sky,
And their gleaming cloud-borne chariots rested on
    the turrets high,

Hero-monarchs, holy Brahmans, filled the halls
    bedecked in gold,
White-robed priests adept in *mantra* mingled with
    the chieftains bold.

And amidst this scene of splendour, pious-hearted,
    pure and good,

Like the sinless god VARUNA, gentle-souled
   Yudhishthir stood,

Six bright fires Yudhishthir lighted, offerings made
   to gods above,
Gifts unto the poor and lowly spake the monarch's
   boundless love.

Hungry men were fed and feasted with an ample
   feast of rice,
Costly gifts to holy Brahmans graced the noble
   sacrifice,

Ida, *ajya*, *homa* offerings, pleased the "Shining
   Ones" on high,
Brahmans pleased with costly presents with their
   blessings filled the sky!

III
GLIMPSES OF THE TRUTH

Dawned the day of *abhisheka*, proud anointment,
   sacred bath,
Crownéd kings and learnéd Brahmans crowded on
   Yudhishthir's path,

And as gods and heavenly *rishis* throng in
    BRAHMA'S mansions bright,
Holy priests and noble monarchs graced the inner
    sacred site!

Measureless their fame and virtue, great their
    penance and their power,
And in converse deep and learned Brahmans
    passed the radiant hour,

And on subjects great and sacred, oft divided in
    their thought,
Various sages in their wisdom various diverse
    maxims taught,

Weaker reasons seemed the stronger, faultless
    reasons often failed,
Keen disputants like the falcon fell on views their
    rivals held!

Some were versed in Laws of Duty, some the Holy
    Vows professed,
Some with gloss and varied comment still his
    learned rival pressed,

Bright the concourse of the Brahmans unto sacred
    learning given,

RAJASUYA

Like the concourse of the bright stars in the
glorious vault of heaven,

None of impure caste and conduct trespassed on
the holy site,
None of impure life and manners stained
Yudhishthir's sacred rite!

Deva-rishi, saintly Narad, marked the
sacrificial rite,
Sanctifying by its lustre good Yudhishthir's royal
might,

And a ray of heavenly wisdom lit the *rishi's*
inner eye,
As he saw the gathered monarchs in the concourse
proud and high!

He had heard from lips celestial in the heavenly
mansions bright,
All these kings were god incarnate, portions of
Celestial Light,

And he saw in them embodied beings of the
upper sky,
And in lotus-eyéd Krishna saw the Highest of
the High!

Saw the ancient World's Preserver, great Creation's
    Primal Cause,
Who had sent the gods as monarchs to uphold his
    righteous laws,

Battle for the cause of virtue, perish in a
    deadly war,
Then to seek their upper mansions in the radiant
    realms afar!

"NARAYANA, world's Preserver, sent immortal
    gods on earth,
He himself in race of Yadu hath assumed his
    mortal birth,

Like the moon among the planets born in Vrishni's
    noble clan,—
He whom bright gods render worship,—
    NARAYANA, Son of Man,

Primal Cause and Self-created! When is done his
    purpose high,
NARAYANA leads Immortals to their dwelling in
    the sky."

Such bright glimpses of the Secret flashed upon
    his inner sight,

As in lofty contemplation Narad gazed upon
   the rite.

IV
THE ARGHYA

Outspake Bhishma to Yudhishthir: "Monarch of
   this wide domain,
Honour due to crownéd monarchs doth our sacred
   law ordain,

Arghya to the wise Preceptor, to the Kinsman and
   to Priest,
To the Friend and to the Scholar, to the King as
   lord of feast,

Unto these is due the *arghya*, so our holy writs
   have said,
Therefore to these kings assembled be the highest
   honour paid,

Noble are these crownéd monarchs, radiant like
   the noonday sun,
To the noblest, first in virtue, be the foremost
   honour done!"

"Who is noblest," quoth Yudhishthir, "in this galaxy of fame,
Who of chiefs and crownéd monarchs doth our foremost honour claim?"

Pond'ring spake the ancient Bhishma in his accents deep and clear:
"Greatest midst the great is Krishna! chief of men without a peer!

Midst these monarchs pure in lustre, purest-hearted and most high
Like the radiant sun is Krishna midst the planets of the sky,

Sunless climes are warmed to verdure by the sun's returning ray,
Windless wastes are waked to gladness when reviving breezes play,

Even so this *rajasuya*, this thy sacrificial rite,
Owes its sanctity and splendour unto Krishna's holy might!"

Bhishma spake and Sahadeva served his mandate quick as thought,

And the *arghya* duly flavoured unto peerless
    Krishna brought,

Krishna trained in rules of virtue then the offered
    arghya took,
Darkened Sisupala's forehead and his frame in
    tremor shook,

To Yudhishthir and to Bhishma turns the chief his
    flaming eyes,
To the great and honoured Krishna, Sisupala
    wrathful cries.

V
SISUPALA'S PRIDE

"Not to Vrishni's uncrowned hero should this
    reverence be paid,
Midst these mighty crownéd monarchs in their
    kingly pomp arrayed,

Ill beseems the good Yudhishthir, royal Pandu's
    righteous son,
Homage to an uncrowned chieftain, to the lowly
    honour done!

Pandu's sons are yet untutored, and with
    knowledge yet unblessed,
Knowing Bhishma blessed with wisdom hath the
    rules of courts transgressed,

Learnéd in the Laws of Duty he hath sinned from
    partial love,
Conscious breach of rules of honour doth our
    deeper hatred move!

In this throng of crownéd monarchs, ruling kings
    of righteous fame,
Can this uncrowned Vrishni chieftain foremost
    rank and honour claim?

Doth he as a sage and elder claim the homage to
    him done?
Sure his father Vasudeva hath his claims before
    his son!

Doth he as Yudhishthir's kinsman count as
    foremost and the best?
Royal Drupad by alliance surely might the claim
    contest!

Doth he as a wise preceptor claim the highest,
    foremost place,

When the great preceptor Drona doth his royal
    mansion grace?

Unto Krishna as a *rishi* should the foremost rank
    be given?
Saintly Vyasa claims the honour, Vedic bard
    inspired by Heaven!

Unto Krishna should we render honour for his
    warlike fame?
Thou, O Bhishma! Death's Subduer, surely might
    precedence claim!

Unto Krishna for his knowledge should the noble
    prize we yield?
Drona's son unmatched in learning surely might
    contest the field!

Great Duryodhan midst the princes stands alone
    without a peer,
Kripa priest of royal Kurus, holiest of all priests
    is here!

Archer Karna—braver archer none there is of
    mortal birth—
Learnt his arms from Par'su Rama, he who slew
    the kings of earth!

Wherefore then to unknown Krishna render we
    this homage free?
Saintly priest, nor wise preceptor, king nor
    foremost chief is he!"

VI
SISUPALA'S FALL

Tiger-hearted Sisupala spake in anger stern
    and high,
Calm unto him Krishna answered, but a light was
    in his eye:

"List, O chiefs and righteous monarchs! From a
    daughter of our race
Evil-destined Sisupala doth his noble lineage trace,

Spite of wrong and frequent outrage, spite of insult
    often flung,
Never in his heart hath Krishna sought to do his
    kinsman wrong!

Once I went to eastern regions, Sisupala like a foe
Burnt my far-famed seaport Dwarka, laid the mart
    and temple low,

RAJASUYA

Once on Bhoja's trusting monarch faithless
   Sisupala fell,
Slew his men and threw him captive in his castle's
   dungeon cell,

Once for holy *aswamedha* Vasudeva sent his steed,
Sisupala stole the charger, sought to stop the
   righteous deed,

Once on saintly Babhru's consort, pious-hearted,
   pure and just,
Sisupala fell in madness, forced the lady to his lust,

Once Visala's beauteous princess went to seek her
   husband's side,
In her husband's garb disguiséd Sisupala clasped
   the bride,

This and more hath Krishna suffered, for his
   mother is our kin,
But the sickening tale appalleth, and he addeth sin
   to sin!

One more tale of sin I mention: by his impious
   passion fired,
To my saintly wife, Rukmini, Sisupala hath
   aspired,

THE MAHABHARATA

As the low-born seeks the *Veda*, soiling it with
     impure breath,
Sisupala sought my consort, and his righteous
     doom is Death!"

Krishna spake; the rising red blood speaks each
     angry hero's shame,
Shame for Chedi's impious actions, grief for
     Sisupala's fame!

Loudly laughed proud Sisupala, spake with bitter
     taunt and jeer,
Answered Krishna's lofty menace with disdain and
     cruel sneer:

"Wherefore in this vast assembly thus proclaim thy
     tale of shame,
If thy wedded wife and consort did inspire my
     youthful flame?

Doth a man of sense and honour, blest with
     wisdom and with pride,
Thus proclaim his wedded consort was another's
     loving bride?

Do thy worst! Or if by anger or by weak
     forbearance led,

RAJASUYA

Sisupala seeks no mercy, nor doth Krishna's anger
    dread!"

Lowered Krishna's eye and forehead, and unto his
    hands there came
Fatal disc, the dread of sinners, disc that never
    missed its aim,

"Monarchs in this hall assembled!" Krishna in his
    anger cried,
"Oft hath Chedi's impious monarch Krishna's
    noble rage defied,

For unto his pious mother plighted word and troth
    was given,
Sisupala's hundred follies would by Krishna be
    forgiven,

I have kept the plighted promise, but his crimes
    exceed the tale,
And beneath this vengeful weapon Sisupala now
    shall quail!"

Then the bright and whirling discus, as this
    mandate Krishna said,
Fell on impious Sisupala, from his body smote
    his head,

Fell the mighty-arméd monarch like a thunder-
   riven rock,
Severed from the parent mountain by the bolt's
   resistless shock!

And his soul be-cleansed of passions came forth
   from its mortal shroud,
Like the radiant sun in splendour from a dark and
   mantling cloud,

Unto Krishna good and gracious, like a lurid spark
   aflame,
Chastened of its sin and anger, Sisupala's spirit
   came!

Rain descends in copious torrents, quick the lurid
   lightnings fly,
And the wide earth feels a tremor, restless
   thunders shake the sky,

Various feelings sway the monarchs as they stand
   in hushed amaze,
Mutely in those speechless moments on the lifeless
   warrior gaze!

Some there are who seek their weapons, and their
   nervous fingers shake,

RAJASUYA

And their lips they bite in anger, and their frames
    in tremor quake,

Others in their inmost bosom welcome Krishna's
    righteous deed,
Look on death of Sisupala as a sinner's proper
    meed,

Rishis bless the deed of Krishna as they wend their
    various ways,
Brahmans pure and pious-hearted chant the
    righteous Krishna's praise!

Sad Yudhishthir, gentle-hearted, thus unto his
    brothers said:
"Funeral rites and regal honours be performed
    unto the dead,"

Duteously his faithful brothers then performed
    each pious rite,
Honours due to Chedi's monarch, to his rank and
    peerless might,

Sisupala's son they seated in his mighty father's
    place,
And with holy *abhisheka* hailed him king of
    Chedi's race!

VII
YUDHISHTHIR EMPEROR

Thus removed the hapless hindrance, now the holy sacrifice
Was performed with joy and splendour and with gifts of gold and rice,

Godlike Krishna watched benignly with his bow and disc and mace,
And Yudhishthir closed the feasting with his kindliness and grace.

Brahmans sprinkled holy water on the empire's righteous lord,
All the monarchs made obeisance, spake in sweet and graceful word:

"Born of race of Ajamidha! thou hast spread thy father's fame,
Rising by thy native virtue thou hast won a mightier name,

And this rite unto thy station doth a holier grace instil,

And thy royal grace and kindness all our hope and
    wish fulfil,

Grant us, king of mighty monarchs, now unto our
    realms we go,
Emperor o'er earthly rulers, blessings and thy
    grace bestow!"

Good Yudhishthir to the monarchs parting grace
    and honours paid,
And unto his duteous brothers thus in loving-
    kindness said:

"To our feast these noble monarchs came from
    loyal love they bear,
Far as confines of their kingdoms, with them let
    our friends repair."

And his brothers and his kinsmen duteously his
    hest obey,
With each parting guest and monarch journey on
    the homeward way,

Arjun wends with high-souled Drupad, famed for
    lofty warlike grace,
Dhrishta-dyumna with Virata, monarch of the
    Matsya race,

Bhima on the ancient Bhishma and on Kuru's king
    doth wait,
Sahadeva waits on Drona, great in arms, in virtue
    great,

With Gandhara's warlike monarch brave Nakula
    holds his way,
Other chiefs with other monarchs where their
    distant kingdoms lay.

Last of all Yudhishthir's kinsman, righteous
    Krishna fain would part,
And unto the good Yudhishthir opens thus his
    joyful heart:

"Done this glorious *rajasuya*, joy and pride of
    Kuru's race,
Grant, O friend! To sea-girt Dwarka, Krishna now
    his steps must trace."

"By thy grace and by thy valour," sad Yudhishthir
    thus replies,
"By thy presence, noble Krishna, I performed this
    high emprise,

By thy all-subduing glory monarchs bore
    Yudhishthir's sway,

RAJASUYA

Came with gifts and costly presents, came their
    tributes rich to pay,

Must thou part? My uttered accents may not bid
    thee, friend, to go,
In thy absence vain were empire, and this life were
    full of woe,

Yet thou partest, sinless Krishna, dearest, best
    belovéd friend,
And to Dwarka's sea-washed mansions Krishna
    must his footsteps bend!"

Then unto Yudhishthir's mother, pious-hearted
    Krishna hies,
And in accents love-inspiring thus to ancient
    Pritha cries:

"Regal fame and righteous glory crown thy sons,
    reveréd dame,
Joy thee in their peerless prowess, in their holy
    spotless fame,

May thy sons' success and triumph cheer a
    widowed mother's heart,
Grant me leave, O noble lady! For to Dwarka I
    depart."

From Yudhishthir's queen Draupadi parts the chief with many a tear,
And from Arjun's wife Sabhadra, Krishna's sister ever dear,

Then with rites and due ablutions to the gods are offerings made,
Priests repeat their benedictions, for the righteous Krishna said,

And his faithful chariot-driver brings his falcon-bannered car,
Like the clouds in massive splendour and resistless in the war,

Pious Krishna mounts the chariot, fondly greets his friends once more,
Leaves blue Jumna's sacred waters for his Dwarka's dear-loved shore.

Still Yudhishthir and his brothers, sad and sore and grieved at heart,
Followed Krishna's moving chariot, for they could not see him part,

Krishna stopped once more his chariot, and his parting blessing gave,

RAJASUYA

Thus the chief with eyes of lotus spake in accents calm and brave:

"*King of men! With sleepless watching ever guard thy kingdom fair,*
Like a father tend thy subjects with a father's love and care,

Be unto them like the rain-drop nourishing the thirsty ground,
Be unto them tree of shelter shading them from heat around,

Like the blue sky ever bending be unto them ever kind,
Free from pride and free from passion rule them with a virtuous mind!"

Spake and left the saintly Krishna, pure and pious-hearted chief,
Sad Yudhishthir wended homeward and his heart was filled with grief.

Book IV
Dyuta
(*The Fatal Dice*)

Duryodhan came back from the Imperial Sacrifice filled with jealousy against Yudhishthir, and devised plans to effect his fall. Sakuni, prince of Gandhara, shared Duryodhan's hatred towards the sons of Pandu, and helped him in his dark scheme.

Yudhishthir with all his piety and righteousness had one weakness, the love of gambling, which was one of the besetting sins of the monarchs of the day. Sakuni was an expert at false dice, and challenged Yudhishthir, and Yudhishthir held it a point of honour not to decline such a challenge.

He came from his new capital, Indra-prastha, to Hastina-pura, the capital of Duryodhan, with his mother and brothers and Draupadi. And as Yudhishthir lost game after game, he was stung with his losses, and with the recklessness of a gambler still went on with the fatal game. His wealth and hoarded gold and jewels, his steeds, elephants and cars, his slaves male and female, his empire and possessions, were all staked and lost!

The madness increased, and Yudhishthir staked

his brothers, and then himself, and then the fair Draupadi, and lost! And thus the Emperor of Indra-prastha and his family were deprived of every possession on earth, and became the bond-slaves of Duryodhan. The old king Dhrita-rashtra released them from actual slavery, but the five brothers retired to forests as homeless exiles.

Portions of Section lxv. and the whole of Sections lxix., lxxvi., and lxxvii. of Book ii. of the original text have been translated in this Book.

I
DRAUPADI IN THE COUNCIL HALL

Glassed on Ganga's limpid waters brightly shine
    Hastina's walls!
Queen Draupadi duly honoured lives within the
    palace halls,

But as steals a lowly jackal in a lordly lion's den,
Base Duryodhan's humble menial came to proud
    Draupadi's ken.

"Pardon, Empress," quoth the menial, "royal
    Pandu's righteous son,
Lost his game and lost his reason, Empress, thou
    art staked and won,

Prince Duryodhan claims thee, lady, and the victor
    bids me say,
Thou shalt serve him as his vassal, as his slave in
    palace stay!"

"Have I heard thee, menial, rightly?" questioned
    she in anguish keen,

"Doth a crownéd king and husband stake his wife
and lose his queen,

Did my noble lord and monarch sense and reason
lose at dice,
Other stake he did not wager, wedded wife to
sacrifice!"

"Other stakes were duly wagered," so he spake
with bitter groan,
"Wealth and empire, every object which
Yudhishthir called his own,

Lost himself and all his brothers, bondsmen are
those princes brave,
Then he staked his wife and empress, thou art
prince Duryodhan's slave!"

Rose the queen in queenly anger, and with
woman's pride she spake:
"Hie thee, menial, to thy master, Queen
Draupadi's answer take,

If my lord, himself a bondsman, then hath staked
his queen and wife,
False the stake, for owns a bondsman neither
wealth nor other's life,

DYUTA

Slave can wager wife nor children, and such action
  is undone,
Take my word to prince Duryodhan, Queen
  Draupadi is unwon!"

Wrathful was the proud Duryodhan when he
  heard the answer bold,
To his younger, wild Duhsasan, this his angry
  mandate told:

"Little-minded is the menial, and his heart in
  terror fails,
For the fear of wrathful Bhima, lo! his coward-
  bosom quails,

Thou Duhsasan, bid the princess as our humble
  slave appear,
Pandu's sons are humble bondsmen, and thy heart
  it owns no fear!"

Fierce Duhsasan heard the mandate, blood-shot
  was his flaming eye,
Forthwith to the inner chambers did with eager
  footsteps hie,

Proudly sat the fair Draupadi, monarch's
  daughter, monarch's wife,

Unto her the base Duhsasan spake the message, insult-rife:

"Lotus-eyed Panchala-princess! fairly staked and won at game,
Come and meet thy lord Duryodhan, chase that mantling blush of shame,

Serve us as thy lords and masters, be our beauteous bright-eyed slave,
Come unto the Council Chamber, wait upon the young and brave!"

Proud Draupadi shakes with tremor at Duhsasan's hateful sight,
And she shades her eye and forehead, and her bloodless cheeks are white,

At his words her chaste heart sickens, and with wild averted eye,
Unto rooms where dwelt the women, Queen Draupadi seeks to fly,

Vainly sped the trembling princess in her fear and in her shame,
By her streaming wavy tresses fierce Duhsasan held the dame!

DYUTA

Sacred locks! With holy water dewed at
    rajasuya rite,
And by *mantra* consecrated, fragrant, flowing,
    raven-bright,

Base Duhsasan by those tresses held the faint and
    flying queen,
Feared no move the sons of Pandu, nor their
    vengeance fierce and keen,

Dragged her in her slipping garments by her long
    and trailing hair,
And like sapling tempest-shaken, wept and shook
    the trembling fair!

Stooping in her shame and anguish, pale with
    wrath and woman's fear,
Trembling and in stifled accents, thus she spake
    with streaming tear:

"Leave me, shameless prince Duhsasan! elders,
    noble lords are here,
Can a modest wedded woman thus in loose attire
    appear?"

Vain the words and soft entreaty which the
    weeping princess made,

Vainly to the gods and mortals she in bitter anguish prayed,

For with cruel words of insult still Duhsasan mocked her woe:
"Loosely clad or void of clothing,—to the council hall you go,

Slave-wench fairly staked and conquered, wait upon thy masters brave,
Live among our household menials, serve us as our willing slave!"

II
DRAUPADI'S PLAINT

Loose-attired, with trailing tresses, came Draupadi weak and faint,
Stood within the Council Chamber, tearful made her piteous plaint:

"Elders! Versed in holy *sastra*, and in every holy rite,
Pardon if Draupadi cometh in this sad unseemly plight,

DYUTA

Stay thy sinful deed, Duhsasan, nameless wrongs
   and insults spare,
Touch me not with hands uncleanly, sacred is a
   woman's hair,

Honoured elders, righteous nobles, have on me
   protection given,
Tremble sinner, seek no mercy from the wrathful
   gods in heaven!

Here in glory, son of DHARMA, sits my noble
   righteous lord,
Sin nor shame nor human frailty stains
   Yudhishthir's deed or word,

Silent all? and will no chieftain rise to save a
   woman's life,
Not a hand or voice is lifted to defend a virtuous
   wife?

Lost is Kuru's righteous glory, lost is Bharat's
   ancient name,
Lost is Kshatra's kingly prowess, warlike worth
   and knightly fame,

Wherefore else do Kuru warriors tamely view this
   impious scene,

Wherefore gleam not righteous weapons to protect
   an outraged queen?

Bhishma, hath he lost his virtue, Drona, hath he
   lost his might,
Hath the monarch of the Kurus ceased to battle
   for the right,

Wherefore are ye mute and voiceless, councillors
   of mighty fame,
Vacant eye and palsied right arm watch this deed
   of Kuru's shame?"

III

INSULT AND VOW OF REVENGE

Spake Draupadi slender-waisted, and her words
   were stern and high,
Anger flamed within her bosom and the tear was
   in her eye,

And her sparkling speaking glances fell on Pandu's
   sons like fire,
Stirred in them a mighty passion and a thirst for
   vengeance dire,

Lost their empire wealth and fortune, little recked
    they for the fall,
But Draupadi's pleading glances like a poniard
    smote them all!

Darkly frowned the ancient Bhishma, wrathful
    Drona bit his tongue,
Pale Vidura marked with anger insults on
    Draupadi flung,

Fulsome word nor foul dishonour could their
    truthful utterance taint,
And they cursed Duhsasan's action, when they
    heard Draupadi's plaint.

But brave Karna, though a warrior,—Arjun's
    deadly foe was he,—
'Gainst the humbled sons of Pandu spake his
    scorn in scornful glee:

"'Tis no fault of thine, fair princess, fallen to this
    servile state,
Wife and son rule not their actions, others rule
    their hapless fate,

Thy Yudhishthir sold his birthright, sold thee at
    the impious play,

And the wife falls with the husband, and her
    duty—to obey!

Live thou in this Kuru household, do the Kuru
    princes' will,
Serve them as thy lords and masters, with thy
    beauty please them still,

Fair One! seek another husband who in foolish
    reckless game
Will not stake a loving woman, will not cast her
    forth in shame!

For they censure not a woman, when she is a
    menial slave,
If her woman's fancy wanders to the young and to
    the brave,

For thy lord is not thy husband, as a slave he hath
    no wife,
Thou art free with truer lover to enjoy a
    wedded life,

They whom at the *swayamvara*, thou had'st chose,
    Panchala's bride,
They have lost thee, sweet Draupadi, lost their
    empire and their pride!"

DYUTA

Bhima heard, and quick and fiercely heaved his
 bosom in his shame,
And his red glance fell on Karna like a tongue of
 withering flame,

Bound by elder's plighted promise Bhima could
 not smite in ire,
Looked the painted form of Anger flaming with an
 anguish dire!

"King and elder!" uttered Bhima, and his words
 were few and brave,
"vain were wrath and righteous passion in the sold
 and bounden slave,

Would that son of chariot-driver fling on us this
 insult keen,
Hadst thou, noble king and elder, staked nor
 freedom nor our queen?"

Sad Yudhishthir heard in anguish, bent in shame
 his lowly head,
Proud Duryodhan laughed in triumph, and in
 scornful accents said:

"Speak, Yudhishthir, for thy brothers own their
 elder's righteous sway,

Speak, for truth in thee abideth, virtue ever marks thy way,

Hast thou lost thy new-built empire, and thy brothers proud and brave,
Hast thou lost thy fair Draupadi, is thy wedded wife our slave?"

Lip nor eye did move Yudhishthir, hateful truth might not deny,
Karna laughed, but saintly Bhishma wiped his old and manly eye.

Madness seized the proud Duryodhan, and inflamed by passion base,
Sought the prince to stain Draupadi with a deep and dire disgrace,

On the proud and peerless woman cast his wicked lustful eye,
Sought to hold the high-born princess as his slave upon his knee!

Bhima penned his wrath no longer, lightning-like his glance he flung,
And the ancient hall of Kurus with his thunder accents rung:

> "May I never reach those mansions where my fathers
>   live on high,
> May I never meet ancestors in the bright and
>   happy sky,
>
> If that knee, by which thou sinnest, Bhima breaks not
>   in his ire,
> In the battle's red arena with his weapon, deathful,
>   dire!"

Red fire flamed on Bhima's forehead, sparkled
    from his angry eye,
As from tough and gnarléd branches fast the
    crackling red sparks fly!

IV

DHRITA-RASHTRA'S KINDNESS

Hark! within the sacred chamber, where the priests
    in white attire
With libations morn and evening feed the
    sacrificial fire,

And o'er sacred rights of *homa* Brahmans chant
    their *mantra* high,

There is heard the jackal's wailing and the raven's
    ominous cry!

Wise Vidura knew that omen, and the Queen
    Gandhari knew,
Bhishma muttered "*svasti! svasti!*" at this portent
    strange and new,

Drona and preceptor Kripa uttered too that
    holy word,
Spake her fears the Queen Gandhari to her spouse
    and royal lord.

Dhrita-rashtra heard and trembled with a sudden
    holy fear,
And his feeble accents quavered, and his eyes were
    dimmed by tear:

"Son Duryodhan, ever luckless, godless, graceless,
    witless child,
Hast thou Drupad's virtuous daughter thus
    insulted and reviled,

Hast thou courted death and danger, for
    destruction clouds our path,
Can an old man's soft entreaties still avert this sign
    of wrath?"

DYUTA

Slow and gently to Draupadi was the sightless
   monarch led,
And in kind and gentle accents unto her the old
   man said:

"Noblest empress, dearest daughter, good
   Yudhishthir's stainless wife,
Purest of the Kuru ladies, nearest to my heart
   and life,

Pardon wrong and cruel insult and avert the wrath
   of Heaven,
Voice thy wish and ask for blessing, be my son's
   misdeed forgiven!"

Answered him the fair Draupadi: "Monarch of the
   Kuru's line,
For thy grace and for thy mercy every joy on earth
   be thine,

Since thou bid'st me name my wishes, this the
   boon I ask of thee,
That my gracious lord Yudhishthir once again be
   bondage-free!

I have borne a child unto him, noble boy and fair
   and brave,

Be he prince of royal station, not the son of
   bounden slave,

Let not light unthinking children point to him in
   utter scorn,
Call him slave and *dasaputra*, of a slave and
   bondsman born!"

"Virtuous daughter, have thy wishes," thus the
   ancient monarch cried,
"Name a second boon and blessing, and it shall be
   gratified."

"Grant me then, O gracious father! mighty Bhima,
   Arjun brave,
And the youngest twin-born brothers,—none of
   them may be a slave

With their arms and with their chariots let the
   noble princes part,
Freemen let them range the country, strong of
   hand and stout of heart!"

"Be it so, high-destined princess!" ancient Dhrita-
   rashtra cried,
"Name another boon and blessing, and it shall be
   gratified,

DYUTA

Foremost of my queenly daughters, dearest-
    cherished and the best,
Meeting thus thy gentle wishes now I feel my
    house is blest!"

"Not so," answered him the princess, "other boon
    I may not seek,
Thou art bounteous, and a woman should be
    modest, wise and meek,

Twice I asked, and twice you granted, and a
    Kshatra asks no more,
Unto Brahmans it is given, asking favours
    evermore,

Now my lord and warlike brothers, from their
    hateful bondage freed,
Seek their fortune by their prowess and by brave
    and virtuous deed!"

V

THE BANISHMENT

Now Yudhishthir 'reft of empire, far from kinsmen,
    hearth and home,

With his wife and faithful brothers must as
    houseless exiles roam,

Parting blessings spake Yudhishthir, "Elder of the
    Kuru line,
Noble grandsire stainless Bhishma, may thy glories
    ever shine,

Drona priest and great preceptor, saintly Kripa
    true and brave,
Kuru's monarch Dhrita-rashtra, may the gods thy
    empire save,

Good Vidura true and faithful, may thy virtue
    serve thee well,
Warlike sons of Dhrita-rashtra, let me bid you all
    farewell!"

So he spake unto his kinsmen, wishing good for
    evil done,
And in silent shame they listened, parting words
    they uttered none,

Pained at heart was good Vidura, and he asked in
    sore distress:
"Noble Pritha, will she wander in the pathless
    wilderness?

DYUTA

Royal-born, unused to hardship, weak and long
   unused to roam,
Agéd is thy saintly mother, let fair Pritha stay
   at home,

And by all beloved, respected, in my house shall
   Pritha dwell,
Till your years of exile over, ye shall greet her safe
   and well."

Answered him the sons of Pandu: "Be it even as
   you say,
Unto us thou art a father, we thy sacred will obey,

Give us then thy holy blessings, friend and father,
   ere we part,
Blessings from the true and righteous brace the
   feeble, fainting heart."

Spake Vidura, pious-hearted: "Best of Bharat's
   ancient race,
Let me bless thee and thy brothers, souls of truth
   and righteous grace,

Fortune brings no weal to mortals who may win
   by wicked wile,

Sorrow brings no shame to mortals who are free
    from sin and guile!

Thou art trained in laws of duty, Arjun is
    unmatched in war,
And on Bhima in the battle kindly shines his
    faithful star,

And the Twins excel in wisdom, born to rule a
    mighty State,
Fair Draupadi, ever faithful, wins the smiles of
    fickle Fate!

Each with varied gifts encircled, each beloved of
    one and all,
Ye shall win a spacious empire, greater, mightier,
    after fall,

And your exile, good Yudhishthir, is ordained to
    serve your weal,
Is a trial and *samadhi*, for it chastens but
    to heal!

Meru taught thee righteous maxims where
    Himalay soars above,
And in Varnavata's forest Vyasa taught thee
    holy love,

DYUTA

Rama preached the laws of duty far on Bhrigu's
   lofty hill,
Sambhu showed the path of virtue by fair Drisad-
   vati's rill,

Fell from lips of saint Asita, words of wisdom deep
   and grave,
Bhrigu touched with fire thy bosom by the dark
   Kalmashi's wave!

Now once more the teaching cometh, purer,
   brighter, oftener taught,
Learn the truth from heavenly Narad, happy is thy
   mortal lot,

Greater than the son of Ila, than the kings of earth
   in might,
Holier than the holy *rishis*, be thou in thy virtue
   bright!

INDRA help thee in thy battles, proud subduer of
   mankind,
YAMA in the mightier duty, in the conquest of
   thy mind,

Good KUVERA teach thee kindness, hungry and
   the poor to feed,

THE MAHABHARATA

King VARUNA quell thy passions, free thy heart
from sin and greed,

Like the Moon in holy lustre, like the Earth in
patience deep,
Like the Sun be full of radiance, strong like Wind's
resistless sweep!

In thy sorrow, in affliction, ever deeper lessons
learn,
Righteous be your life in exile, happy be your safe
return,

May these eyes again behold thee in Hastina's
ancient town,
Conqueror of earthly trials, crowned with virtue's
heavenly crown!"

Spake Vidura to the brothers, and they felt their
might increase,
Bowed to him in salutation, filled with deeper,
holier peace,

Bowed to Bhishma and to Drona, and to chiefs
and elders all,
Exiles to the pathless jungle left their father's
ancient hall!

VI
PRITHA'S LAMENT

In the inner palace chambers where the royal
>ladies dwell,
Unto Pritha came Draupadi, came to speak her
>sad farewell,

Monarch's daughter, monarch's consort, as an
>exile she must go,
Pritha wept and in the chambers rose the wailing
>voice of woe!

Heaving sobs convulsed her bosom as a silent
>prayer she prayed,
And in accents choked by anguish thus her parting
>words she said:

"Grieve not, child, if bitter fortune so ordains that
>we must part,
Virtue hath her consolations for the true and
>loving heart,

And I need not tell thee, daughter, duties of a
>faithful wife,

Drupad's and thy husband's mansions thou hast
  brightened by thy life!

Nobly from the sinning Kurus thou hast turned
  thy righteous wrath,
Safely, with a mother's blessing, tread the trackless
  jungle path,

Dangers bring no woe or sorrow to the true and
  faithful wife,
Sinless deed and holy conduct ever guard her
  charméd life,

Nurse thy lord with woman's kindness, and his
  brothers, where ye go,
Young in years in Sahadeva, gentle and unused
  to woe!"

"May thy blessings help me, mother," so the fair
  Draupadi said,
"Safe in righteous truth and virtue, forest paths we
  fearless tread!"

Wet her eyes and loose her tresses, fair Draupadi
  bowed and left,
Ancient Pritha weeping followed of all earthly joy
  bereft,

DYUTA

As she went, her duteous children now before their
      mother came,
Clad in garments of the deer-skin, and their heads
      were bent in shame!

Sorrow welling in her bosom choked her voice and
      filled her eye,
Till in broken stifled accents faintly thus did
      Pritha cry:

"Ever true to path of duty, noble children void of
      stain,
True to gods, to mortals faithful, why this
      undeservéd pain,

Wherefore hath untimely sorrow like a darksome
      cloud above,
Cast its pale and deathful shadow on the children
      of my love?

Woe to me, your wretched mother, woe to her who
      gave you birth,
Stainless sons, for sins of Pritha have ye suffered
      on this earth,

Shall ye range the pathless forest dreary day and
      darksome night,

'Reft of all save native virtue, clad in native, inborn might?

Woe to me, from rocky mountains where I dwelt by Pandu's side,
When I lost him, to Hastina wherefore came I in my pride,

Happy is your sainted father, dwells in regions of the sky,
Sees nor feels these earthly sorrows gathering on us thick and high,

Happy too is faithful Madri, for she trod the virtuous way,
Followed Pandu to the bright sky, and is now his joy and stay!

Ye alone are left to Pritha, dear unto her joyless heart,
Mother's hope and widow's treasure, and ye may not, shall not part,

Leave me not alone on wide earth, loving sons, your virtues prove,
Dear Draupadi, loving daughter, let a mother's tear-drops move,

DYUTA

Grant me mercy, kind Creator, and my days in
   mercy close,
End my sorrows, kind VIDHATA, end my life with
   all my woes!

Help me, pious-hearted Krishna, friend of
   friendless, wipe my pain,
All who suffer pray unto thee and they never pray
   in vain,

Help me, Bhishma, warlike Drona, Kripa ever
   good and wise,
Ye are friends of truth and virtue, righteous truth
   ye ever prize,

Help me from thy starry mansions, husband,
   wherefore dost thou wait,
Seest thou not thy godlike children exiled by a
   bitter fate!

Part not, leave me not, my children, seek ye not
   the trackless way,
Stay but one, if one child only, as your mother's
   hope and stay,

Youngest, gentlest Sahadeva, dearest to this
   widowed heart,

Wilt thou watch beside thy mother, while thy cruel
　　brothers part?"

Whispering words of consolation, Pritha's children
　　wiped her tear,
Then unto the pathless jungle turned their
　　footsteps lone and drear!

Kuru dames with fainting Pritha to Vidura's
　　palace hie,
Kuru queens for weeping Pritha raise their voice in
　　answering cry,

Kuru maids for fair Draupadi fortune's fitful will
　　upbraid,
And their tear-dewed lotus-faces with their
　　streaming fingers shade,

Dhrita-rashtra, ancient monarch, is by sad
　　misgivings pained,
Questions oft with anxious bosom what the cruel
　　fates ordained.

Book V
Pativrata-Mahatmya
(*Woman's Love*)

True to their word the sons of Pandu went with Draupadi into exile, and passed twelve years in the wilderness; and many were the incidents which checkered their forest life. Krishna, who had stood by Yudhishthir in his prosperity, now came to visit him in his adversity; he consoled Draupadi in her distress, and gave good advice to the brothers. Draupadi with a woman's pride and anger still thought of her wrongs and insults, and urged Yudhishthir to disregard the conditions of exile and recover his kingdom. Bhima too was of the same mind, but Yudhishthir would not be moved from his plighted word.

The great *rishi* Vyasa came to visit Yudhishthir, and advised Arjun, great archer as he was, to acquire celestial arms by penance and worship. Arjun followed the advice, met the god SIVA in the guise of a hunter, pleased him by his prowess in combat, and obtained his blessings and the *pasupata* weapon. Arjun then went to INDRA'S heaven and obtained other celestial arms.

In the meanwhile Duryodhan, not content with sending his cousins to exile, wished to humiliate them still more by appearing before them in all his regal power and splendour. Matters however turned out differently from what he expected, and he became involved in a quarrel with some *gandharvas*, a class of aerial beings. Duryodhan was taken captive by them, and it was the Pandav brothers who released him from his captivity, and allowed him to return to his kingdom in peace. This act of generosity rankled in his bosom and deepened his hatred.

Jayadratha, king of the Sindhu or Indus country, and a friend and ally of Duryodhan, came to the woods, and in the absence of the Pandav brothers carried off Draupadi. The Pandavs however pursued the king, chastised him for his misconduct, and rescued Draupadi.

Still more interesting than these various incidents are the tales and legends with which this book is replete. Great saints came to see Yudhishthir in his exile, and narrated to him legends of ancient times and of former kings. One of these beautiful episodes, the tale of Nala and Damayanti, has been translated into graceful English verse by Dean Milman, and is known to many English readers. The legend of Agastya who drained the ocean dry; of Parasu-Rama a

PATIVRATA-MAHATMYA

Brahman who killed the Kshatriyas of the earth; of Bhagiratha who brought down the Ganges from the skies to the earth; of Manu and the universal deluge; of Vishnu and various other gods; of Rama and his deeds which form the subject of the Epic *Ramayana*;—these and various other legends have been interwoven in the account of the forest-life of the Pandavs, and make it a veritable storehouse of ancient Hindu tales and traditions.

Among these various legends and tales I have selected one which is singular and striking. The great truth proclaimed under the thin guise of an eastern allegory is that a True Woman's Love is not conquered by Death. The story is known by Hindu women high and low, rich and poor, in all parts of India; and on a certain night in the year millions of Hindu women celebrate a rite in honour of the woman whose love was not conquered by death. Legends like these, though they take away from the unity and conciseness of the Epic, impart a moral instruction to the millions of India the value of which cannot be overestimated.

The portion translated in this Book forms Sections ccxcii. and ccxciii., a part of Section ccxciv. and Sections ccxcv. and ccxcvi. of Book iii. of the original text.

I
FOREST LIFE

In the dark and pathless forest long the Pandav
    brothers strayed,
In the bosom of the jungle with the fair Draupadi
    stayed,

And they killed the forest red-deer, hewed the
    gnarléd forest wood,
From the stream she fetched the water, cooked the
    humble daily food,

In the morn she swept the cottage, lit the cheerful
    fire at eve,
But at night in lonesome silence oft her woman's
    heart would grieve,

Insults rankled in her bosom and her tresses were
    unbound,—
So she vowed,—till fitting vengeance had the base
    insulters found!

Oft when evening's shades descended, mantling
    o'er the wood and lea,

PATIVRATA-MAHATMYA

When Draupadi by the cottage cooked the food beneath the tree,

Rishis came to good Yudhishthir, sat beside his evening fires,
Many olden tales recited, legends of our ancient sires.

Markandeya, holy *rishi*, once unto Yudhishthir came,
When his heart was sorrow-laden with the memories of his shame,

"Pardon, father!" said Yudhishthir, "if unbidden tears will start,
But the woes of fair Draupadi grieve a banished husband's heart,

By her tears the saintly woman broke my bondage worse than death,
By my sins she suffers exile and misfortune's freezing breath!

Dost thou, sage and saintly *rishi*, know of wife or woman born,
By such nameless sorrow smitten, by such strange misfortune torn,

Hast thou in thy ancient legends heard of true and
 faithful wife,
With a stronger wife's affection, with a sadder
 woman's life?"

"Listen, monarch!" said the *rishi*, "to a tale of
 ancient date,
How Savitri loved and suffered, how she strove
 and conquered Fate!"

II
THE TALE OF SAVITRI

In the country of fair Madra lived a king in days
 of old,
Faithful to the holy BRAHMA, pure in heart and
 righteous-souled,

He was loved in town and country, in the court
 and hermit's den,
Sacrificer to the bright gods, helper to his
 brother men,

But the monarch, Aswapati, son or daughter had
 he none,

PATIVRATA-MAHATMYA

Old in years and sunk in anguish, and his days
    were almost done!

Vows he took and holy penance, and with pious
    rules conformed,
Spare in diet as *brahmachari* many sacred rites
    performed,

Sang the sacred hymn, *savitri*, to the gods
    oblations gave,
Through the lifelong day he fasted,
    uncomplaining, meek and brave!

Year by year he gathered virtue, rose in merit and
    in might,
Till the goddess of *savitri* smiled upon his
    sacred rite,

From the fire upon the altar which a holy radiance
    flung,
In the form of beauteous maiden, goddess of
    savitri sprung!

And she spake in gentle accents, blessed the
    monarch good and brave,
Blessed his rites and holy penance and a boon
    unto him gave:

"Penance and thy sacrifices can the Powers
  Immortal move,
And the pureness of thy conduct doth thy heart's
  affection prove,

Ask thy boon, king Aswapati, from creation's
  Ancient Sire,
True to virtue's sacred mandate speak thy inmost
  heart's desire."

"For an offspring brave and kingly," so the saintly
  king replied,
"Holy rites and sacrifices and this penance I have
  tried,

If these rites and sacrifices move thy favour and
  thy grace,
Grant me offspring, Prayer-Maiden, worthy of my
  noble race."

"Have thy object," spake the maiden, "Madra's
  pious-hearted king,
From SWAYMBHU, Self-created, blessings unto
  thee I bring,

For HE lists to mortal's prayer springing from a
  heart like thine,

PATIVRATA-MAHATMYA

And HE wills,—a noble daughter grace thy famed
   and royal line,

Aswapati, glad and grateful, take the blessing
   which I bring,
Part in joy and part in silence, bow unto Creation's
   King!"

Vanished then the Prayer-Maiden, and the king of
   noble fame,
Aswapati, Lord of coursers, to his royal city came,

Days of hope and nights of gladness Madra's
   happy monarch passed,
Till his queen of noble offspring gladsome promise
   gave at last!

As the moon each night increaseth chasing
   darksome nightly gloom,
Grew the unborn babe in splendour in its happy
   mother's womb,

And in fullness of the season came a girl with
   lotus-eye,
Father's hope and joy of mother, gift of kindly
   gods on high!

And the king performed its birth-rites with a glad
and grateful mind,
And the people blessed the dear one with their
wishes good and kind,

As *Savitri*, Prayer-Maiden, had the beauteous
offspring given,
Brahmans named the child *Savitri*, holy gift of
bounteous Heaven!

Grew the child in brighter beauty like a goddess
from above,
And each passing season added fresher sweetness,
deeper love,

Came with youth its lovelier graces, as the buds
their leaves unfold,
Slender waist and rounded bosom, image as of
burnished gold,

Deva-Kanya! born a goddess, so they said in all
the land,
Princely suitors struck with splendour ventured
not to seek her hand.

Once upon a time it happened on a bright and
festive day,

PATIVRATA-MAHATMYA

Fresh from bath the beauteous maiden to the altar
   came to pray,

And with cakes and pure libations duly fed the
   Sacred Flame,
Then like SRI in heavenly radiance to her royal
   father came.

And she bowed to him in silence, sacred flowers
   beside him laid,
And her hands she folded meekly, sweetly her
   obeisance made,

With a father's pride, upon her gazed the ruler of
   the land,
But a strain of sadness lingered, for no suitor
   claimed her hand.

"Daughter," whispered Aswapati, "now, methinks,
   the time is come,
Thou shouldst choose a princely suitor, grace a
   royal husband's home,

Choose thyself a noble husband worthy of thy
   noble hand,
Choose a true and upright monarch, pride and
   glory of his land,

As thou choosest, gentle daughter, in thy loving
    heart's desire,
Blessing and his free permission will bestow thy
    happy sire.

For our sacred *sastras* sanction, holy Brahmans oft
    relate,
That the duty-loving father sees his girl in wedded
    state,

That the duty-loving husband watches o'er his
    consort's ways,
That the duty-loving offspring tends his mother's
    widowed days,

Therefore choose a loving husband, daughter of
    my house and love,
So thy father earn no censure or from men or gods
    above."

Fair Savitri bowed unto him and for parting
    blessings prayed,
Then she left her father's palace and in distant
    regions strayed,

With her guard and aged courtiers whom her
    watchful father sent,

Mounted on her golden chariot unto sylvan
    woodlands went.

Far in pleasant woods and jungle wandered she
    from day to day,
Unto *asrams*, hermitages, pious-hearted held
    her way,

Oft she stayed in holy *tirthas* washed by sacred
    limpid streams,
Food she gave unto the hungry, wealth beyond
    their fondest dreams,

Many days and months are over, and it once did
    so befall,
When the king and *rishi* Narad sat within the
    royal hall,

From her journeys near and distant and from
    places known to fame,
Fair Savitri with the courtiers to her father's
    palace came,

Came and saw her royal father, *rishi* Narad by
    his seat,
Bent her head in salutation, bowed unto their
    holy feet.

THE MAHABHARATA

III
THE FATED BRIDEGROOM

"Whence comes she," so Narad questioned,
    "whither was Savitri led,
Wherefore to a happy husband hath Savitri not
    been wed?"

"Nay, to choose her lord and husband," so the
    virtuous monarch said,
"Fair Savitri long hath wandered and in holy
    tirthas stayed,

Maiden! Speak unto the *rishi*, and thy choice and
    secret tell,"
Then a blush suffused her forehead, soft and slow
    her accents fell!

"Listen, father! Salwa's monarch was of old a king
    of might,
Righteous-hearted Dyumat-sena, feeble now and
    void of sight,

Foemen robbed him of his kingdom when in age
    he lost his sight,

PATIVRATA-MAHATMYA

And from town and spacious empire was the
 monarch forced to flight,

With his queen and with his infant did the feeble
 monarch stray,
And the jungle was his palace, darksome was his
 weary way,

Holy vows assumed the monarch and in penance
 passed his life,
In the wild woods nursed his infant and with wild
 fruits fed his wife,

Years have gone in rigid penance, and that child is
 now a youth,
Him I choose my lord and husband, Satyavan, the
 Soul of Truth!"

Thoughtful was the *rishi* Narad, doleful were the
 words he said:
"Sad disaster waits Savitri if this royal youth
 she wed,

Truth-beloving is his father, truthful is the royal
 dame,
Truth and virtue rule his actions, Satyavan his
 sacred name,

Steeds he loved in days of boyhood and to paint
    them was his joy,
Hence they called him young Chitraswa, art-
    beloving gallant boy,

But O pious-hearted monarch! Fair Savitri hath
    in sooth
Courted Fate and sad disaster in that noble gallant
    youth!"

"Tell me," questioned Aswapati, "for I may not
    guess thy thought,
Wherefore is my daughter's action with a sad
    disaster fraught,

Is the youth of noble lustre, gifted in the gifts
    of art,
Blest with wisdom and with prowess, patient in his
    dauntless heart?"

"SURYA'S lustre in him shineth," so the *rishi*
    Narad said,
"BRIHASPATI'S wisdom dwelleth in the youthful
    prince's head,

Like MAHENDRA in his prowess, and in patience
    like the Earth,

PATIVRATA-MAHATMYA

Yet O king! a sad disaster marks the gentle youth
    from birth!"

"Tell me, *rishi*, then thy reason," so the anxious
    monarch cried,
"Why to youth so great and gifted may this maid
    be not allied,

Is he princely in his bounty, gentle-hearted in his
    grace,
Duly versed in sacred knowledge, fair in mind and
    fair in face?"

"Free in gifts like Rantideva," so the holy *rishi* said,
"Versed in lore like monarch Sivi who all ancient
    monarchs led,

Like Yayati open-hearted and like CHANDRA in his
    grace,
Like the handsome heavenly ASVINS fair and
    radiant in his face,

Meek and graced with patient virtue he controls
    his noble mind,
Modest in his kindly actions, true to friends and
    ever kind,

And the hermits of the forest praise him for his
  righteous truth,
Nathless, king, thy daughter may not wed this
  noble-hearted youth!"

"Tell me, *rishi*," said the monarch, "for thy sense
  from me is hid,
Has this prince some fatal blemish, wherefore is
  this match forbid?"

"Fatal fault!" exclaimed the *rishi*, "fault that
  wipeth all his grace,
Fault that human power nor effort, rite nor
  penance can efface,

Fatal fault or destined sorrow! for it is decreed
  on high,
On this day, a twelve-month later, this ill-fated
  prince will die!"

Shook the startled king in terror and in fear and
  trembling cried:
"Unto short-lived, fated bridegroom ne'er my
  child shall be allied,

Come, Savitri, dear-loved maiden, choose another
  happier lord,

PATIVRATA-MAHATMYA

Rishi Narad speaketh wisdom, list unto his
   holy word!

Every grace and every virtue is effaced by
   cruel Fate,
On this day, a twelve-month later, leaves the prince
   his mortal state!"

"Father!" answered thus the maiden, soft and sad
   her accents fell,
"I have heard thy honoured mandate, holy Narad
   counsels well,

Pardon witless maiden's fancy, but beneath the eye of
   Heaven,
Only once a maiden chooseth, twice her troth may not
   be given,

Long his life or be it narrow, and his virtues great
   or none,
Satyavan is still my husband, he my heart and troth
   hath won,

What a maiden's heart hath chosen that a maiden's
   lips confess,
True to him thy poor Savitri goes into the wilderness!"

"Monarch!" uttered then the *rishi*, "fixed is she in
   mind and heart,
From her troth the true Savitri never, never will
   depart,

More than mortal's share of virtue unto Satyavan
   is given,
Let the true maid wed her chosen, leave the rest to
   gracious Heaven!"

"*Rishi* and preceptor holy!" so the weeping
   monarch prayed,
"Heaven avert all future evils, and thy mandate is
   obeyed!"

Narad wished him joy and gladness, blessed the
   loving youth and maid,
Forest hermits on their wedding every fervent
   blessing laid.

IV

OVERTAKEN BY FATE

Twelve-month in the darksome forest by her true
   and chosen lord,

PATIVRATA-MAHATMYA

Sweet Savitri served his parents by her thought
    and deed and word,

Bark of tree supplied her garments draped upon
    her bosom fair,
Or the red cloth as in *asrams* holy women love
    to wear.

And the aged queen she tended with a fond and
    filial pride,
Served the old and sightless monarch like a
    daughter by his side,

And with love and gentle sweetness pleased her
    husband and her lord,
But in secret, night and morning, pondered still on
    Narad's word!

Nearer came the fatal morning by the holy
    Narad told,
Fair Savitri reckoned daily and her heart was still
    and cold,

Three short days remaining only! and she took a
    vow severe
Of *triratra*, three nights' penance, holy fasts and
    vigils drear.

Of Savitri's rigid penance heard the king with
   anxious woe,
Spake to her in loving accents, so the vow she
   might forgo:

"Hard the penance, gentle daughter, and thy
   woman's limbs are frail,
After three nights' fasts and vigils sure thy tender
   health may fail,"

"Be not anxious, loving father," meekly this Savitri
   prayed,
"Penance I have undertaken, will unto the gods be
   made."

Much misdoubting then the monarch gave his sad
   and slow assent,
Pale with fast and unseen tear-drops, lonesome
   nights Savitri spent,

Nearer came the fatal morning, and to-morrow he
   shall die,
Dark, lone hours of nightly silence! Tearless,
   sleepless is her eye!

"Dawns that dread and fated morning!" said
   Savitri, bloodless, brave,

PATIVRATA-MAHATMYA

Prayed her fervent prayers in silence, to the Fire
    oblations gave,

Bowed unto the forest Brahmans, to the parents
    kind and good,
Joined her hands in salutation and in reverent
    silence stood.

With the usual morning blessing, *"Widow may'st
    thou never be,"*
Anchorites and agéd Brahmans blessed Savitri
    fervently,

O! that blessing fell upon her like the rain on
    thirsty air,
Struggling hope inspired her bosom as she drank
    those accents fair,

But returned the dark remembrance of the *rishi*
    Narad's word,
Pale she watched the creeping sun beams, mused
    upon her fated lord!

"Daughter, now thy fast is over," so the loving
    parents said,
"Take thy diet after penance, for thy morning
    prayers are prayed,"

THE MAHABHARATA

"Pardon, father," said Savitri, "let this other day be done,"
Unshed tear-drops filled her eyelids, glistened in the morning sun!

Satyavan, sedate and stately, ponderous axe on shoulder hung,
For the distant darksome jungle issued forth serene and strong,

But unto him came Savitri and in sweetest accents prayed,
As upon his manly bosom gently she her forehead laid:

"Long I wished to see the jungle where steals not the solar ray,
Take me to the darksome forest, husband, let me go to-day!"

"Come not, love," he sweetly answered with a loving husband's care,
"Thou art all unused to labour, forest paths thou may'st not dare,

And with recent fasts and vigils pale and bloodless is thy face,

And thy steps are weak and feeble, jungle paths
 thou may'st not trace."

"Fasts and vigils make me stronger," said the wife
 with wifely pride,
"Toil I shall not feel nor languor when my lord is
 by my side,

For I feel a woman's longing with my lord to trace
 the way,
Grant me, husband ever gracious, with thee let me
 go to-day!"

Answered then the loving husband, as his hands in
 hers he wove,
"Ask permission from my parents in the trackless
 woods to rove,"

Then Savitri to the monarch urged her longing
 strange request,
After duteous salutation thus her humble prayer
 addrest.

"To the jungle goes my husband, fuel and the fruit
 to seek,
I would follow if my mother and my loving father
 speak,

Twelve-month from this narrow *asram* hath Savitri
    stepped nor strayed,
In this cottage true and faithful ever hath Savitri
    stayed,

For the sacrificial fuel wends my lord his
    lonesome way,
Please my kind and loving parents, I would follow
    him to-day."

"Never since her wedding morning," so the loving
    king replied,
"Wish or thought Savitri whispered, for a boon or
    object sighed,

Daughter, thy request is granted, safely in the
    forest roam,
Safely with thy lord and husband seek again thy
    cottage home."

Bowing to her loving parents did the fair Savitri
    part,
Smile upon her pallid features, anguish in her
    inmost heart,

Round her sylvan greenwoods blossomed 'neath a
    cloudless Indian sky,

PATIVRATA-MAHATMYA

Flocks of pea-fowls gorgeous plumaged flew
    before her wondering eye,

Woodland rills and crystal nullahs gently roll'd
    o'er rocky bed,
Flower-decked hills in dewy brightness towering
    glittered overhead,

Birds of song and beauteous feather trilled a note
    in every grove,
Sweeter accents fell upon her, from her husband's
    lips of love!

Still with thoughtful eye Savitri watched her dear
    and fated lord,
Flail of grief was in her bosom but her pale lips
    shaped no word,

And she listened to her husband still on anxious
    thought intent,
Cleft in two her throbbing bosom as in silence still
    she went!

Gaily with the gathered wild-fruits did the prince
    his basket fill,
Hewed the interlacéd branches with his might and
    practiced skill,

Till the drops stood on his forehead, weary was his aching head,
Faint he came unto Savitri and in faltering accents said:

"Cruel ache is on my forehead, fond and ever faithful wife,
And I feel a hundred needles pierce me and torment my life,

And my feeble footsteps falter and my senses seem to reel,
Fain would I beside thee linger for a sleep doth o'er me steal."

With a wild and speechless terror pale Savitri held her lord,
On her lap his head she rested as she laid him on the sward,

Narad's fatal words remembered as she watched her husband's head,
Burning lip and pallid forehead and the dark and creeping shade,

Clasped him in her beating bosom, kissed his lips with panting breath,

Darker grew the lonesome forest, and he slept the
 sleep of death!

V

TRIUMPH OVER FATE

In the bosom of the shadows rose a Vision dark
 and dread,
Shape of gloom in inky garment and a crown was
 on his head,

Gleaming form of sable splendour, blood-red was
 his sparkling eye,
And a fatal noose he carried, grim and godlike,
 dark and high!

And he stood in solemn silence, looked in silence
 on the dead,
And Savitri on the greensward gently placed her
 husband's head,

And a tremor shook Savitri, but a woman's love is
 strong,
With her hands upon her bosom thus she spake
 with quivering tongue:

"More than mortal is thy glory! If a radiant god
    thou be,
Tell me what bright name thou bearest, what thy
    message unto me."

"Know me," thus responded YAMA, "mighty
    monarch of the dead,
Mortals leaving earthly mansion to my darksome
    realms are led.

Since with woman's full affection thou hast loved
    thy husband dear,
Hence before thee, faithful woman, YAMA doth in
    form appear,

But his days and loves are ended, and he leaves his
    faithful wife,
In this noose I bind and carry spark of his
    immortal life,

Virtue graced his life and action, spotless was his
    princely heart,
Hence for him I came in person, princess, let thy
    husband part."

YAMA from the prince's body, pale and bloodless,
    cold and dumb,

PATIVRATA-MAHATMYA

Drew the vital spark, *purusha*, smaller than the human thumb,

In his noose the spark he fastened, silent went his darksome way,
Left the body shorn of lustre to its rigid cold decay,

Southward went the dark-hued YAMA with the youth's immortal life,
And, for woman's love abideth, followed still the faithful wife.

"Turn, Savitri," outspake YAMA, "for thy husband loved and lost,
Do the rites due unto mortals by their Fate predestined crost,

For thy wifely duty ceases, follow not in fruitless woe,
And no farther living creature may with monarch YAMA go!"

"But I may not choose but follow where thou takest my husband's life,
For Eternal Law divides not loving man and faithful wife,

For a woman's true affection, for a woman's
    sacred woe,
Grant me in thy godlike mercy farther still with
    him I go!

Fourfold are our human duties: first to study
    holy lore,
Then to live as good householders, feed the
    hungry at our door,

Then to pass our days in penance, last to fix our
    thoughts above,
But the final goal of virtue, it is Truth and
    deathless Love!"

"True and holy are thy precepts," listening YAMA
    made reply,
"And they fill my heart with gladness and with
    pious purpose high,

I would bless thee, fair Savitri, but the dead come
    not to life,
Ask for other boon and blessing, faithful, true and
    virtuous wife!"

"Since you so permit me, YAMA," so the good
    Savitri said,

PATIVRATA-MAHATMYA

"For my husband's banished father let my dearest suit be made,

Sightless in the darksome forest dwells the monarch faint and weak,
Grant him sight and grant him vigour, YAMA, in thy mercy speak!"

"Duteous daughter," YAMA answered, "be thy pious wishes given,
And his eyes shall be restoréd to the cheerful light of heaven,

Turn, Savitri, faint and weary, follow not in fruitless woe,
And no farther living creature may with monarch YAMA go!"

"Faint nor weary is Savitri," so the noble princess said,
"Since she waits upon her her husband, gracious Monarch of the dead,

What befalls the wedded husband still befalls the faithful wife,
Where he leads she ever follows, be it death or be it life!

And our sacred writ ordaineth and our pious
    rishis sing,
Transient meeting with the holy doth its countless
    blessings bring,

Longer friendship with the holy purifies the mortal
    birth,
Lasting union with the holy is the bright sky on the
    earth,

Union with the pure and holy is immortal
    heavenly life,
For Eternal Law divides not loving man and
    faithful wife!"

"Bless*é*d are thy words," said YAMA, "bless*é*d is thy
    pious thought,
With a higher purer wisdom are thy holy lessons
    fraught,

I would bless thee, fair Savitri, but the dead come
    not to life,
Ask for other boon and blessing, faithful, true and
    virtuous wife!"

"Since you so permit me, YAMA," so the good
    Savitri said,

PATIVRATA-MAHATMYA

"Once more for my husband's father be my
  supplication made,

Lost his kingdom, in the forest dwells the monarch
  faint and weak,
Grant him back his wealth and kingdom, YAMA, in
  thy mercy speak!"

"Loving daughter," YAMA answered, "wealth and
  kingdom I bestow,
Turn, Savitri, living mortal may not with King
  YAMA go!"

Still Savitri, meek and faithful, followed her
  departed lord,
YAMA still with higher wisdom listened to her
  saintly word,

And the Sable King was vanquished, and he
  turned on her again,
And his words fell on Savitri like the cooling
  summer rain,

"Noble woman, speak thy wishes, name thy boon
  and purpose high,
What the pious mortal asketh gods in heaven may
  not deny!"

"Thou hast," so Savitri answered, "granted father's realm and might,
To his vain and sightless eyeballs hast restored their blessèd sight,

Grant him that the line of monarchs may not all untimely end,
Satyavan may see his kingdom to his royal sons descend!"

"Have thy object," answered YAMA, "and thy lord shall live again,
He shall live to be a father, and his children too shall reign,

For a woman's troth abideth longer than the fleeting breath,
And a woman's love abideth higher than the doom of Death!"

VI
RETURN HOME

Vanished then the Sable Monarch, and Savitri
    held her way
Where in dense and darksome forest still her
    husband lifeless lay,

And she sat upon the greensward by the cold
    unconscious dead,
On her lap with deeper kindness placed her
    consort's lifeless head,

And that touch of true affection thrilled him back
    to waking life,
As returned from distant regions gazed the prince
    upon his wife,

"Have I lain too long and slumbered, sweet Savitri,
    faithful spouse,
But I dreamt a Sable Person took me in a fatal
    noose!"

"Pillowed on this lap," she answered, "long upon
    the earth you lay,

And the Sable Person, husband, he hath come and
    passed away,

Rise and leave this darksome forest if thou feelest
    light and strong,
For the night is on the jungle and our way is dark
    and long."

Rising as from happy slumber looked the young
    prince on all around,
Saw the wide-extending jungle mantling all the
    darksome ground,

"Yes," he said, "I now remember, ever loving
    faithful dame,
We in search of fruit and fuel to this lonesome
    forest came,

As I hewed the gnarléd branches, cruel anguish
    filled my brain,
And I laid me on the greensward with a throbbing
    piercing pain,

Pillowed on thy gentle bosom, solaced by thy
    gentle love,
I was soothed, and drowsy slumber fell on me
    from skies above.

PATIVRATA-MAHATMYA

All was dark and then I witnessed, was it but a
　　fleeting dream,
God or Vision, dark and dreadful, in the deepening
　　shadows gleam,

Was this dream my fair Savitri, dost thou of this
　　Vision know,
Tell me, for before my eyesight still the Vision
　　seems to glow!"

"Darkness thickens," said Savitri, "and the evening
　　waxeth late,
When the morrow's light returneth I shall all these
　　scenes narrate,

Now arise, for darkness gathers, deeper grows the
　　gloomy night,
And thy loving anxious parents trembling wait thy
　　welcome sight,

Hark the rangers of the forest! How their voices
　　strike the ear,
Prowlers of the darksome jungle! How they fill my
　　breast with fear!

Forest-fire is raging yonder, for I see a distant
　　gleam,

And the rising evening breezes help the red and
    radiant beam,

Let me fetch a burning faggot and prepare a
    friendly light,
With these fallen withered branches chase the
    shadows of the night,

And if feeble still thy footsteps,—long and weary is
    our way,—
By the fire repose, my husband, and return by light
    of day."

"For my parents, fondly anxious," Satyavan thus
    made reply,
"Pains my heart and yearns my bosom, let us to
    their cottage hie,

When I tarried in the jungle or by day or dewy eve,
Searching in the hermitages often did my parents
    grieve,

And with father's soft reproaches and with
    mother's loving fears,
Chid me for my tardy footsteps, dewed me with
    their gentle tears.

PATIVRATA-MAHATMYA

Think then of my father's sorrow, of my mother's
    woeful plight,
If afar in wood and jungle pass we now the livelong
    night,

Wife beloved, I may not fathom what mishap or
    load of care,
Unknown dangers, unseen sorrows, even now my
    parents share!"

Gentle drops of filial sorrow trickled down his
    manly eye,
Fond Savitri sweetly speaking softly wiped the
    tear-drops dry:

"Trust me, husband, if Savitri hath been faithful in
    her love,
If she hath with pious offerings served the
    righteous gods above,

If she hath a sister's kindness unto brother men
    performed,
If she hath in speech and action unto holy truth
    conformed,

Unknown blessings, mighty gladness, trust thy
    ever faithful wife,

And not sorrows or disasters wait this eve our
  parents' life!"

Then she rose and tied her tresses, gently helped
  her lord to rise,
Walked with him the pathless jungle, looked with
  love into his eyes,

On her neck his clasping left arm sweetly winds in
  soft embrace,
Round his waist Savitri's right arm doth as sweetly
  interlace,

Thus they walked the darksome jungle, silent stars
  looked from above,
And the hushed and throbbing midnight watched
  Savitri's deathless love.

Book VI
Go-Harana
(Cattle-Lifting)

The conditions of the banishment of the sons of Pandu were hard. They must pass twelve years in exile, and then they must remain a year in concealment. If they were discovered within this last year, they must go into exile for another twelve years.

Having passed the twelve years of exile in forests, the Pandav brothers disguised themselves and entered into the menial service of Virata, king of the Matsyas, to pass the year of concealment. Yudhishthir presented himself as a Brahman, skilled in dice, and became a courtier of the king. Bhima entered the king's service as cook. For Arjun, who was so well known, a stricter concealment was necessary. He wore conch bangles and earrings and braided his hair, like those unfortunate beings whom nature has debarred from the privileges of men and women, and he lived in the inner apartments of the king. He assumed the name of *Brihannala*, and taught the inmates of the royal household in music and dancing. Nakula became a keeper of the king's horses, and

Sahadeva took charge of the king's cows. Draupadi too disguised herself as a waiting-woman, and served the princess of the Matsya house in that humble capacity.

In these disguises the Pandav brothers safely passed a year in concealment in spite of all search which Duryodhan made after them. At last an incident happened which led to their discovery when the year was out.

Cattle-lifting was a common practice with the kings of ancient India, as with the chiefs of ancient Greece. The king of the Trigartas and the king of the Kurus combined and fell on the king of the Matsyas in order to drive off the numerous herds of fine cattle for which his kingdom was famed. The Trigartas entered the Matsya Kingdom from the south-east, and while Virata went out with his troops to meet the foe, Duryodhan with his Kuru forces fell on the kingdom from the north.

When news came that the Kurus had invaded the kingdom, there was no army in the capital to defend it. King Virata had gone out with most of his troops to face the Trigartas in the south-east, and the prince Uttara had no inclination to face the Kurus in the north. The disguised Arjun now came to the rescue in the manner described in this Book. The description of the bows, arrows, and swords of the Pandav brothers which they had concealed in a tree, wrapped like human corpses to frighten away inquisitive travellers, throws some light on the arts and manufactures of ancient times. The portions translated in this Book form Sections xxxv., xxxvi., xl. to xliii., a portion of Section xliv., and Sections liii. and lxxii. of Book iv. of the original text.

I
COMPLAINT OF THE COWHERD

Monarch of the mighty Matsyas, brave Virata
 known to fame,
Marched against Trigarta chieftains who from
 southward regions came,

From the north the proud Duryodhan, stealing
 onwards day by day,
Swooped on Matsya's fattened cattle like the hawk
 upon its prey!

Bhishma, Drona, peerless Karna, led the Kuru
 warriors brave,
Swept the kingdom of Virata like the ocean's
 surging wave,

Fell upon the trembling cowherds, chased them
 from the pasture-field,
Sixty thousand head of cattle was the Matsya
 country's yield!

And the wailing chief of cowherds fled forlorn,
 fatigued and spent,

GO-HARANA

Speeding on his rapid chariot to the royal
    city went,

Came inside the city portals, came within the
    palace gate,
Struck his forehead in his anguish and bewailed
    his luckless fate.

Meeting there the prince Uttara, youth of beauty
    and of fame,
Told him of the Kurus' outrage and lamented
    Matsya's shame:

"Sixty thousand head of cattle, bred of Matsya's
    finest breed,
To Hastina's distant empire do the Kuru
    chieftains lead,

Glory of the Matsya nation! Save thy father's
    valued kine,
Quick thy footsteps, strong thy valour, vengeance
    deep and dire be thine!

'Gainst the fierce Trigarta chieftains Matsya's
    warlike king is gone,
Thee we count our lord and saviour as our
    monarch's gallant son,

THE MAHABHARATA

Rise, Uttara! beat the Kurus, homeward lead the
  stolen kine,
Like an elephant of jungle, pierce the Kurus'
  shattered line!

As the *Vina* speaketh music, by musicians tuned
  aright,
Let thy sounding bow and arrows speak thy deeds
  of matchless might,

Harness quick thy milk-white coursers to thy
  sounding battle-car,
Hoist thy golden lion-banner, speed thee, prince,
  unto the war!

And as thunder-wielding INDRA smote *Asuras*
  fierce and bold,
Smite the Kurus with thy arrows winged with
  plumes of yellow gold

As the famed and warlike Arjun is the stay of
  Kuru's race,
Thou art refuge of the Matsyas and thy kingdom's
  pride and grace!"

But the prince went not to battle from the foe to
  guard the State,

GO-HARANA

To the cowherd answered gaily, sheltered by the palace gate:

"Not unknown to me the usage of the bow and wingéd dart,
Not unknown the warrior's duty or the warrior's noble art,

I would win my father's cattle from the wily foeman's greed,
If a skillful chariot-driver could my fiery coursers lead.

For my ancient chariot-driver died on battle's gory plain,
Eight and twenty days we wrestled, many warlike chiefs were slain,

Bring me forth a skillful driver who can urge the battle-steed,
I will hoist my lion-banner, to the dubious battle speed.

Dashing through the foeman's horses, ranks of elephant and car,
I will win the stolen cattle rescued in the field of war,

And like thunder-wielding INDRA, smiting Danu's
    sons of old,
I will smite the Kuru chieftains, drive them to their
    distant hold!

Bhishma and the proud Duryodhan, archer Karna
    known to fame,
Drona too shall quail before me and retreat in
    bitter shame,

For those warriors in my absence Matsya's far-
    famed cattle steal,
But beneath my countless arrows Matsya's
    vengeance they shall feel,

Bring me forth a chariot-driver, let me speed my
    battle-car,
And in wonder they will question—Is this Arjun
    famed in war?"

II

THE DISGUISED CHARIOTEER

Arjun, guised as Brihannala, heard the boast
    Uttara made,

GO-HARANA

And to try his skill and valour thus to fair
    Draupadi prayed:

"Say to him that Brihannala will his battle-chariot
    lead,
That as Arjun's chariot-driver he hath learned to
    urge the steed,

Say that faithful Brihannala many a dubious war
    hath seen,
And will win his father's cattle in this contest fierce
    and keen."

Fair Draupadi, guised as menial, Arjun's secret
    hest obeyed,
Humbly stepped before Uttara and in gentle
    accents prayed:

"Hear me, prince, yon Brihannala will thy battle-
    chariot lead,
He was Arjun's chariot-driver, skilled to urge the
    flying steed,

Trained in war by mighty Arjun, trained to drive
    the battle-car,
He hath followed helmèd Arjun in the glorious
    field of war,

And when Arjun conquered Khandav, this, Uttara,
  I have seen,
Brihannala drove his chariot, for I served
  Yudhishthir's queen."

Heard Uttara hesitating, spake his faint and timid
  mind,
"I would trust thee, beauteous maiden, lotus-
  bosomed, ever kind,

But a poor and sexless creature, can he rein the
  warlike steed,
Can I ask him, worse than woman, in the battle's
  ranks to lead?"

"Need is none," Draupadi answered, "Brihannala's
  grace to ask,
He is eager like the war-horse for this great and
  warlike task,

And he waits upon thy sister, she will bid the
  minion speed,
And he wins thy father's cattle, and the victor's
  glorious meed!"

Matsya's princess spake to Arjun, Arjun led the
  battle-car,

Led the doubting prince Uttara to the dread and
>   dubious war.

III
ARMS AND WEAPONS

Arjun drove the prince of Matsya to a darksome
>   *sami* tree,
Spake unto the timid warrior in his accents bold
>   and free:

"Prince, thy bow and shining arrows, pretty
>   handsome toys are these,
Scarcely they beseem a warrior, and a warrior
>   cannot please,

Thou shalt find upon this *sami*, mark my words
>   which never fail,
Stately bows and wingéd arrows, banners, swords
>   and coats of mail,

And a bow which strongest warriors scarce can in
>   the battle bend,
And the limits of a kingdom widen when that bow
>   is strained,

THE MAHABHARATA

Tall and slender like a palm-tree, worthy of a warrior bold,
Smooth the wood of hardened fibre, and the ends are yellow gold!"

Doubting still Uttara answered: "In this *sami's* gloomy shade
Corpses hang since many seasons in their wrappings duly laid,

Now I mark them all suspended, horrent, in the open air,
And to touch the unclean objects, friend, is more than I can dare!"

"Fear not warrior," Arjun answered, "for the tree conceals no dead,
Warriors' weapons, cased like corpses, lurk within its gloomy shade,

And I ask thee, prince of Matsya, not to touch an unclean thing,
But unto a chief and warrior weapons and his arms to bring."

Prince Uttara gently lighted, climbed the dark and leafy tree,

GO-HARANA

Arjun from the prince's chariot bade him speed
the arms to free,

And the young prince cut the wrappings; lo! the
shining bows appear
Twisted, voiced like hissing serpents, like the
bright stars glistening clear!

Seized with wonder prince Uttara silently the
weapons eyed,
And unto his chariot-driver thus in trembling
accents cried:

"Whose this bow so tall and stately, speak to me
my gentle friend,
On the wood are golden bosses, tipped with gold is
either end,

Whose this second ponderous weapon stout and
massive in the hold,
On the staff are worked by artists elephants of
burnished gold,

And what great and mighty monarch owns this
other bow of might,
Set with golden glittering insects on its ebon back
so bright,

Golden suns of wondrous brightness on this fourth
their lustre lend,
Who may be the unknown archer who this stately
bow can bend,

And the fifth is set with jewels, gems and stones of
purest ray,
Golden fire-flies glint and sparkle in the yellow
light of day!

Who doth own these shining arrows with their
heads in gold encased,
Thousand arrows bright and feathered in the
golden quivers placed,

Next are these with vulture-feather, golden-yellow
in their hue,
Made of iron keen and whetted, whose may be
these arrows true,

Next upon this sable quiver jungle tigers gleam
in gold,
And these keen and boar-eared arrows speak some
chieftain fierce and bold,

Fourth are these seven hundred arrows, crescent
in their shining blade,

GO-HARANA

Thirsting for the blood of foemen and by cunning
   artists made,

And the fifth are golden-crested, made of
   tempered steel and bright,
Parrot feathers wing these arrows whetted and of
   wondrous might!

Mark again this wondrous sabre, shape of toad is
   on the hilt,
On the blade a toad is given and the scabbard
   nobly gilt,

Larger, stouter is this second in its sheath of
   tiger-skin,
Decked with bells and gold-surmounted and the
   blade is bright and keen,

Next this scimitar so curious by the skilled
   Nishadas made,
Scabbard made of wondrous cowhide sheathes the
   bright and polished blade,

Fourth, a long and beauteous weapon glittering
   sable in its hue,
With its sheath of softer goat-skin worked with
   gold on azure blue,

And the fifth is broad and massive over thirty
    fingers long,
Golden-sheathed and gold embosséd like a snake
    or fiery tongue!"

Joyously responded Arjun: "Mark this bow
    embossed with gold.
'Tis the wondrous bow, *Gandiva*, worthy of a
    warrior bold,

Gift of heaven! to archer Arjun kindly gods this
    weapon sent,
And the confines of a kingdom widen when the
    bow is bent,

Next, this mighty ponderous weapon worked with
    elephants of gold,
With this bow the stalwart Bhima hath the tide of
    conquests rolled,

And the third with golden insects by a cunning
    hand inlaid,
'Tis Yudhishthir's royal weapon by the noblest
    artists made,

Next the bow with solar lustre brave Nakula wields
    in fight,

GO-HARANA

And the fifth is Sahadeva's, decked with gems and
 jewels bright!

Mark again these thousand arrows, unto Arjun
 they belong,
And the darts whose blades are crescent unto
 Bhima brave and strong,

Boar-ear shafts are young Nakula's, in the tiger-
 quiver cased,
Sahadeva owns the arrows with the parrot's feather
 graced,

These three-knotted shining arrows, thick and
 yellow vulture-plumed.
They belong to King Yudhishthir, with their heads
 by gold illumed!

Listen more, if of these sabres, prince of Matsya,
 thou wouldst know,
Arjun's sword is toad-engraven, ever dreaded by
 the foe,

And the sword in tiger-scabbard, massive and of
 mighty strength,
None save tiger-waisted Bhima wields that sword
 of wondrous length,

Next the sabre golden-hilted, sable and with gold
    embossed,
Brave Yudhishthir kept that sabre when the king
    his kingdom lost,

Yonder sword with goat-skin scabbard brave
    Nakula wields in war,
In the cowhide Sahadeva keeps his shining
    scimitar!"

"Strange thy accents," spake Uttara, "stranger are
    the weapons bright,
Are they arms of sons of Pandu famed on earth for
    matchless might,

Where are now those pious princes by a dire
    misfortune crossed,
Warlike Arjun, good Yudhishthir, by his subjects
    loved and lost,

Where is tiger-waisted Bhima, matchless fighter in
    the field,
And the brave and twin-born brothers skilled the
    arms of war to wield?

O'er a game they lost their empire and we heard of
    them no more,

GO-HARANA

Or perchance they lonesome wander on some wild
    and distant shore,

And Draupadi noble princess, purest best of
    womankind,
Doth she wander with Yudhishthir, changeless in
    her heart and mind?"

Proudly answered valiant Arjun, and a smile was
    on his face,
"Not in distant lands the brothers do their
    wandering footsteps trace,

In thy father's court disguiséd lives Yudhishthir just
    and good,
Bhima in thy father's palace as a cook prepares
    the food,

Brave Nakula guards the horses, Sahadeva tends
    the kine,
As thy sister's waiting-woman doth the fair
    Draupadi shine,

Pardon, prince, these rings and bangles, pardon strange
    unmanly guise,
'Tis no poor and sexless creature,—Arjun greets thy
    wondering eyes!"

IV
RESCUE OF THE CATTLE

Arjun decked his mighty stature in the gleaming
 arms of war,
And with voice of distant thunder rolled the
 mighty battle-car,

And the Kurus marked with wonder Arjun's
 standard lifted proud,
Heard with dread the deep *Gandiva* sounding oft
 and sounding loud,

And they knew the wondrous bowman wheeling
 round the battle-car,
And with doubts and grave misgivings whispered
 Drona skilled in war:

"That is Arjun's monkey-standard, how it greets
 my ancient eyes,
Well the Kurus know the standard like a comet in
 the skies,

Hear ye not the deep *Gandiva?* How my ear its
 accents greet,

GO-HARANA

Mark ye not these pointed arrows falling prone
  before my feet,

By these darts his salutation to his teacher loved
  of old,
Years of exile now completed, Arjun sends with
  greetings bold!

How the gallant prince advances! Now I mark his
  form and face,
Issuing from his dark concealment with a brighter,
  haughtier grace,

Well I know his bow and arrows and I know his
  standard well,
And the deep and echoing accents of his far-
  resounding shell,

In his shining arms accoutred, gleaming in his
  helmet dread,
Shines he like the flame of *homa* by libations
  duly fed!"

Arjun marked the Kuru warriors arming for th'
  impending war,
Whispered thus to prince Uttara as he drove the
  battle-car:

"Stop thy steeds, O prince of Matsya! for too close
  we may not go,
Stop thy chariot whence my arrows reach and slay
  the distant foe,

Seek we out the Kuru monarch, proud Duryodhan
  let us meet,
If he falls we win the battle, other chieftains will
  retreat.

There is Drona my preceptor, Drona's warlike son
  is there,
Kripa and the mighty Bhishma, archer Karna tall
  and fair,

Them I seek not in this battle, lead, O lead thy
  chariot far,
Midst the chiefs Duryodhan moves not, moves not
  in the ranks of war,

But to save the pilfered cattle speeds he onward in
  his fear,
While these warriors stay and tarry to defend their
  monarch's rear,

But I leave these car-borne warriors, other work
  to-day is mine,

GO-HARANA

Meet Duryodhan in the battle, win thy father's
    stolen kine!"

Matsya's prince then turned the courses, left
    behind the war's array,
Where Duryodhan with the cattle quickly held his
    onward way,

Kripa marked the course of Arjun, guessed his
    inmost thought aright,
Thus he spake to brother warriors urging speed
    and instant fight:

"Mark ye, chieftains, gallant Arjun wheels his
    sounding battle-car,
'Gainst our prince and proud Duryodhan seeks to
    turn the tide of war,

Let us fall upon our foeman and our prince and
    leader save,
Few save INDRA, god of battles, conquers Arjun
    fierce and brave,

What were Matsya's fattened cattle, many
    thousands though they be,
If our monarch sinks in battle like a ship in
    stormy sea!"

Vain were Kripa's words of wisdom, Arjun drove
    the chariot fair,
While his shafts like countless locusts whistled
    through the ambient air,

Kuru soldiers struck with panic neither stood and
    fought, nor fled,
Gazed upon the distant Arjun, gazed upon their
    comrades dead!

Arjun twanged his mighty weapon, blew his far-
    resounding shell,
Strangely spake his monkey-standard, Kuru
    warriors knew it well,

Sankha's voice, *Gandiva's* accents, and the
    chariot's booming sound,
Filled the air like distant thunder, shook the firm
    and solid ground.

Kuru soldiers fled in terror or they slumbered with
    the dead,
And the rescued lowing cattle with their tails
    uplifted fled!

GO-HARANA

V

WARRIOR'S GUERDON

Now with joy the king Virata to his royal city came,
Saw the rescued herds of cattle, saw Uttara prince
    of fame,

Marked the great and gallant Arjun, helmet-
    wearing, armour-cased,
Knew Yudhishthir and his brothers now as royal
    princes dressed,

And he greeted good Yudhishthir, truth-beloving
    brave and strong,
And to valiant Arjun offered Matsya's princess fair
    and young!

"Pardon, monarch," answered Arjun, "but I may
    not take as bride,
Matsya's young and beauteous princess whom I
    love with father's pride,

She hath often met me trusting in the inner
    palace hall,
As a daughter on a father waited on my loving call!

I have trained her *kokil* accents, taught her maiden steps in dance,
Watched her skill and varied graces all her native charms enhance,

Pure is she in thought and action, spotless as my hero boy,
Grant her to my son, O monarch, as his wedded wife and joy!

Abhimanyu trained in battle, handsome youth of godlike face,
Krishna's sister, fair Subhadra, bore the child of princely grace,

Worthy of thy youthful daughter, pure in heart and undefiled,
Grant it, sire, my Abhimanyu wed thy young and beauteous child!"

Answered Matsya's noble monarch with a glad and grateful heart:
"Words like these befit thy virtue, nobly hast thou done thy part,

Be it as thou sayest, Arjun, unto Pandu's race allied,

Matsya's royal line is honoured, Matsya's king is
>   gratified!"

VI
THE WEDDING

Good Yudhishthir heard the tidings and he gave
>   his free assent,
Unto distant chiefs and monarchs kindly
>   invitations sent,

In the town of Upa-plavya, of fair Matsya's towns
>   the best,
Made their home the pious brothers to receive
>   each royal guest.

Came unto them Kasi's monarch and his arméd
>   troopers came,
And the king of fair Panchala with his sons of
>   warlike fame,

Came the sons of fair Draupadi early trained in art
>   of war,
Other chiefs and sacrifices came from regions near
>   and far.

Krishna decked in floral garlands with his elder
 brother came,
And his sister fair Subhadra, Arjun's loved and
 longing dame,

Arjun's son brave Abhimanyu came upon his
 flowery car,
With his elephants and chargers, troopers trained
 in art of war.

Vrishnis from the sea-girt Dwarka, brave
 Andhakas known to fame,
Bhojas from the mighty Chumbal with the
 righteous Krishna came,

He to gallant sons of Pandu made his presents rich
 and rare,
Gems and gold and costly garments, slaves and
 damsels passing fair.

With its quaint and festive greetings came at last
 the bridal day,
Matsya maids were merry-hearted, Pandu's sons
 were bright and gay,

Conch and cymbal, horn and trumpet spake forth
 music soft and sweet

GO-HARANA

In Virata's royal palace, in the peopled mart and
    street!

And they slay the jungle red-deer, and they spread
    the ample board,
And prepare the cooling palm-drink with the
    richest viands stored,

Mimes and actors please the people, bards recite
    the ancient song,
Glories of heroic houses minstrels by their lays
    prolong!

And deep-bosomed dames of Matsya, jasmine-
    form and lotus-face,
With their pearls and golden garlands joyously the
    bridal grace,

Circled by those royal ladies, though they all are
    bright and fair,
Brightest shines the fair Draupadi with a beauty
    rich and rare,

Stately dames and merry maidens lead the young
    and soft-eyed bride,
As the queens of gods encircle INDRA'S daughter
    in her pride!

Arjun from the Matsya monarch takes the princess
    passing fair,
For his son by fair Subhadra, nursed by Krishna's
    loving care,

With a godlike grace Yudhishthir stands by faithful
    Arjun's side,
As a father takes a daughter, takes the young and
    beauteous bride,

Joins her hands to Abhimanyu's, and with cake
    and parchéd rice,
On the altar brightly blazing doth the holy
    sacrifice.

Matsya's monarch on the bridegroom rich and
    costly presents pressed,
Elephants he gave two hundred, steeds seven
    thousand of the best,

Poured libations on the altar, on the priests
    bestowed his gold,
Offered to the sons of Pandu rich domain and
    wealth untold.

With a pious hand Yudhishthir, true in heart and
    pure in mind,

GO-HARANA

Made his gifts in gold and garments, kine and
 wealth of every kind,

Costly chariots, beds of splendour, robes with
 thread of gold belaced,
Viands rich and sweet confection, drinks the
 richest and the best,

Lands he gave unto the Brahman, bullocks to the
 labouring swain,
Steeds he gave unto the warrior, to the people gifts
 and grain,

And the city of the Matsyas, teeming with a wealth
 untold,
Shone with festive joy and gladness and with flags
 and cloth of gold.

Book VII
Udyoga
(*The Council of War*)

The term of banishment having expired, Yudhishthir demanded that the kingdom of Indra-prastha should be restored to him. The old Dhrita-rashtra and his queen and the aged and virtuous councillors advised the restoration, but the jealous Duryodhan hated his cousins with a genuine hatred, and would not consent. All negotiations were therefore futile, and preparations were made on both sides for the most sanguinary and disastrous battle that had ever been witnessed in Northern India.

The portions translated in this Book are from Sections i., ii., iii., xciv., cxxiv., and cxxvi. of Book v. of the original text.

I
KRISHNA'S SPEECH

Mirth and song and nuptial music waked the
    echoes of the night,
Youthful bosoms throbbed with pleasure, lovelit
    glances sparkled bright,

But when young and white-robed USHAS ope'd the
    golden gates of day,
To Virata's council chamber chieftains thoughtful
    held their way,

Stones inlaid in arch and pillar glinted in the
    glittering dawn,
Gay festoons and graceful garlands o'er the golden
    cushions shone!

Matsya's king, Panchala's monarch, foremost seats
    of honour claim,
Krishna too and Valadeva, Dwarka's chiefs of
    righteous fame,

By them sat the bold Satyaki from the sea-girt
    western shore,

UDYOGA

And the godlike sons of Pandu,—days of dark
concealment o'er,

Youthful princes in their splendour graced Virata's
royal hall,
Valiant sons of valiant fathers, brave in war, august
and tall,

In their gem-bespangled garments came the
warriors proud and high,
Till the council chamber glittered like the star-
bespangled sky!

Kind the greetings, sweet the converse, soft the
golden moments fly,
Till intent on graver questions all on Krishna turn
their eye,

Krishna with his inner vision then the state of
things surveyed,
And his thoughts before the monarchs thus in
weighty accents laid:

"Known to all, ye mighty monarchs! May your
glory ever last,
True to plighted word Yudhishthir hath his weary
exile passed,

Twelve long years with fair Draupadi in the
>   pathless jungle strayed,
And a year in menial service in Virata's palace
>   stayed,

He hath kept his plighted promise, braved
>   affliction, woe, and shame,
And he begs, assembled monarchs, ye shall now
>   his duty name.

For he swerveth not from duty kingdom of the sky
>   to win,
Prizeth hamlet more than empire, so his course be
>   free from sin,

Loss of realm and wealth and glory higher virtues
>   in him prove,
Thoughts of peace and not of anger still the good
>   Yudhishthir move!

Mark again the sleepless anger and the unrelenting
>   hate
Harboured by the proud Duryodhan driven by his
>   luckless fate,

From a child, by fire or poison, impious guile or
>   trick of dice,

UDYOGA

He hath compassed dark destruction by deceit and
  low device!

Ponder well, ye gracious monarchs, with a just and
  righteous mind,
Help Yudhishthir with your counsel, with your
  grace and blessings kind,

Should the noble son of Pandu seek his right by
  open war,
Seek the aid of righteous monarchs and of
  chieftains near and far?

Should he smite his ancient foemen skilled in each
  deceitful art,
Unforgiving in their vengeance, unrelenting in
  their heart?

Should he rather send a message to the proud
  unbending foe,
And Duryodhan's haughty purpose seek by
  messenger to know?

Should he send a noble envoy, trained in virtue,
  true and wise,
With his greetings to Duryodhan in a meek and
  friendly guise?

Ask him to restore the kingdom on the sacred
    Jumna's shore,
Either king may rule his empire as in happy days
    of yore?"

Krishna uttered words of wisdom pregnant with
    his peaceful thought,
For in peace and not by bloodshed still
    Yudhishthir's right he sought.

II
VALADEVA'S SPEECH

Krishna's elder Valadeva, stalwart chief who bore
    the plough,
Rose and spake, the blood of Vrishnis mantled o'er
    his lofty brow:

"Ye have listened, pious monarchs, to my brother's
    gentle word,
Love he bears to good Yudhishthir and to proud
    Hastina's lord,

For his realm by dark blue Jumna good
    Yudhishthir held of yore,

UDYOGA

Brave Duryodhan ruled his kingdom on the ruddy
    Ganga's shore,

And once more in love and friendship either
    prince may rule his share,
For the lands are broad and fertile, and each realm
    is rich and fair!

Speed the envoy to Hastina with our love and
    greetings kind,
Let him speak Yudhishthir's wishes, seek to know
    Duryodhan's mind,

Make obeisance unto Bhishma and to Drona true
    and bold,
Unto Kripa, archer Karna, and to chieftains young
    and old,

To the sons of Dhrita-rashtra, rulers of the Kuru
    land,
Righteous in their kingly duties, stout of heart and
    strong of hand,

To the princes and to burghers gathered in the
    council hall,
Let him speak Yudhishthir's wishes, plead
    Yudhishthir's cause to all.

Speak he not in futile anger, for Duryodhan holds
  the power,
And Yudhishthir's wrath were folly in this sad and
  luckless hour,

By his dearest friends dissuaded, but by rage or
  madness driven,
He hath played and lost his empire, may his folly
  be forgiven!

Indra-prastha's spacious empire now Duryodhan
  deems his own,
By his tears and soft entreaty let Yudhishthir seek
  the throne,

Open war I do not counsel, humbly seek
  Duryodhan's grace,
War will not restore the empire nor the gambler's
  loss replace!"

Thus with cold and cruel candour stalwart
  Valadeva cried,
Wrathful rose the brave Satyaki, fiercely thus to
  him replied.

III
SATYAKI'S SPEECH

"Shame unto the halting chieftain who thus pleads
 Duryodhan's part,
Timid counsel, Valadeva, speaks a woman's timid
 heart,

Oft from warlike stock ariseth weakling chief who
 bends the knee,
As a withered fruitless sapling springeth from a
 fruitful tree!

From a heart so faint and craven, faint and craven
 words must flow,
Monarchs in their pride and glory list not to such
 counsel low,

Couldst thou, impious Valadeva, midst these
 potentates of fame,
On Yudhishthir pious-hearted cast this undeservéd
 blame?

Challenged by his wily foeman and by dark
 misfortune crost,

Trusting to their faith Yudhishthir played a
  righteous game and lost,

Challenge from a crownéd monarch can a
  crownéd king decline,
Can a Kshatra warrior fathom fraud in sons of
  royal line?

Nathless he surrendered empire true to faith and
  plighted word,
Lived for years in pathless forests Indra-prastha's
  mighty lord,

Past his years of weary exile, now he claims his
  realm of old,
Claims it, not as humble suppliant, but as king and
  warrior bold,

Past his year of dark concealment, bold
  Yudhishthir claims his own,
Proud Duryodhan now must render Indra-
  prastha's jewelled throne!

Bhishma counsels, Drona urges, Kripa pleads for
  right in vain,
False Duryodhan will not render sinful conquest,
  fraudful gain,

UDYOGA

Open war I therefore counsel, ruthless and
    relentless war,
Grace we seek not when we meet them speeding in
    our battle-car!

And our weapons, not entreaties, shall our foemen
    force to yield,
Yield Yudhishthir's rightful kingdom or they perish
    on the field,

False Duryodhan and his forces fall beneath our
    battle's shock,
As beneath the bolt of thunder falls the crushed
    and riven rock!

Who shall meet the helméd Arjun in the gory field
    of war,
Krishna with his fiery discus mounted on his
    battle-car,

Who shall face the twin-born brothers by the
    mighty Bhima led,
And the vengeful chief Satyaki with his bow and
    arrows dread?

Ancient Drupad wields his weapon peerless in the
    field of fight,

And his brave son, born of AGNI, owns an all-
    consuming might,

Abhimanyu, son of Arjun, whom the fair Subhadra
    bore,
And whose happy nuptials brought us from far
    Dwarka's sea-girt shore,

Men on earth nor bright Immortals can the
    youthful hero face,
When with more than Arjun's prowess Abhimanyu
    leads the race!

Dhrita-rashtra's sons we conquer and Gandhara's
    wily son,
Vanquish Karna though world-honoured for his
    deeds of valour done,

Win the fierce-contested battle and redeem
    Yudhishthir's own,
Place the exile pious-hearted on his father's
    ancient throne!

And no sin Satyaki reckons slaughter of the
    mortal foe,
But to beg a grace of foemen were a mortal sin
    and woe,

Speed we then unto our duty, let our impious
    foemen yield,
Or the fiery son of Sini meets them on the
    battle-field!"

IV

DRUPAD'S SPEECH

Fair Panchala's ancient monarch rose his secret
    thoughts to tell,
From his lips the words of wisdom with a graceful
    accent fell:

"Much I fear thou speakest truly, hard is Kuru's
    stubborn race,
Vain the hope, the effort futile, to beseech
    Duryodhan's grace!

Dhrita-rashtra pleadeth vainly, feeble is his
    fitful star,
Ancient Bhishma, righteous Drona, cannot stop
    this fatal war,

Archer Karna thirsts for battle, moved by jealousy
    and pride,

Deep Sakuni, false and wily, still supports
  Duryodhan's side!

Vain is Valadeva's counsel, vainly shall our envoy
  plead,
Half his empire proud Duryodhan yields not in his
  boundless greed,

In his pride he deems our mildness faint and
  feeble-hearted fear,
And our suit will fan his glory and his arrogance
  will cheer!

Therefore let our many heralds travel near and
  travel far,
Seek alliance of all monarchs in the great
  impending war,

Unto brave and noble chieftains, unto nations east
  and west,
North and south to warlike races speed our
  message and request!

Meanwhile peace and offered friendship we before
  Duryodhan place,
And my priest will seek Hastina, strive to win
  Duryodhan's grace,

UDYOGA

If he renders Indra-prastha, peace will crown the
>happy land,
Or our troops will shake the empire from the east
>to western strand!"

Vainly were Panchala's Brahmans sent with
>messages of peace,
Vainly urged the Kuru elders that the fatal feud
>should cease,

Proud Duryodhan to his kinsmen would not yield
>their proper share,
Pandu's sons would not surrender, for they had
>the will to dare!

Fatal war and dire destruction did the mighty gods
>ordain,
Till the kings and arméd nations strewed the red
>and reeking plain,

Krishna in his righteous effort sought for wisdom
>from above,
Strove to stop the war of nations and to end the
>feud in love,

And to far Hastina's palace Krishna went to sue
>for peace,

Raised his voice against the slaughter, begged that
 strife and feud should cease!

V

KRISHNA'S SPEECH AT HASTINA

Silent sat the listening chieftains in Hastina's
 council hall,
With the voice of rolling thunder Krishna spake
 unto them all:

"Listen, mighty Dhrita-rashtra, Kuru's great and
 ancient king,
Seek not war and death of kinsmen, word of peace
 and love I bring!

'Midst the wide earth's many nations Bharats in
 their worth excel,
Love and kindness, spotless virtue, in the Kuru-
 elders dwell,

Father of the noble nation, now retired from life's
 turmoil,
Ill beseems that sin or untruth should thy ancient
 bosom soil!

For thy sons in impious anger seek to do their
    kinsmen wrong,
And withhold the throne and kingdom which by
    right to them belong,

And a danger thus ariseth like the comet's baleful
    fire,
Slaughtered kinsmen, bleeding nations, soon shall
    feed its fatal ire!

Stretch thy hands, O Kuru monarch! prove thy
    truth and holy grace,
Man of peace! avert the slaughter and preserve thy
    ancient race,

Yet restrain thy fiery children, for thy mandates
    they obey,
I with sweet and soft persuasion Pandu's truthful
    sons will sway.

'Tis thy profit, Kuru monarch! that the fatal feud
    should cease,
Brave Duryodhan, good Yudhishthir, rule in
    unmolested peace,

Pandu's sons are strong in valour, mighty in their
    arméd hand,

INDRA shall not shake thy empire when they guard
the Kuru land!

Bhishma is thy kingdom's bulwark, doughty Drona
rules the war,
Karna matchless with his arrows, Kripa peerless in
his car,

Let Yudhishthir and stout Bhima by these noble
warriors stand,
And let helmet-wearing Arjun guard the sacred
Kuru land,

Who shall then contest thy prowess from the sea to
farthest sea,
Ruler of a worldwide empire, king of kings and
nations free?

Sons and grandsons, friends and kinsmen, will
surround thee in a ring,
And a race of loving heroes guard their ancient
hero-king,

Dhrita-rashtra's lofty edicts will proclaim his
boundless sway,
Nations work his righteous mandates and the
kings his will obey!

If this concord be rejected and the lust of war
    prevail,
Soon within these ancient chambers will resound
    the sound of wail,

Grant thy children be victorious and the sons of
    Pandu slain,
Dear to thee are Pandu's children, and their death
    must cause thee pain!

But the Pandavs skilled in warfare are renowned
    both near and far,
And thy race and children's slaughter will
    methinks pollute this war,

Sons and grandsons, loving princes, thou shalt
    never see again,
Kinsmen brave and car-borne chieftains will
    bedeck the gory plain!

Ponder yet, O ancient monarch! Rulers of each
    distant State,
Nations from the farthest regions gather thick to
    court their fate,

Father of a righteous nation! Save the princes of
    the land,

On the armed and fated nations stretch, old man,
    thy saving hand!

Say the word, and at thy bidding leaders of each
    hostile race
Not the gory field of battle but the festive board
    will grace,

Robed in jewels, decked in garlands, they will
    quaff the ruddy wine,
Greet their foes in mutual kindness, bless thy holy
    name and thine!

Think, O man of many seasons! When good Pandu
    left this throne,
And his helpless loving orphans thou didst cherish
    as thine own,

'Twas thy helping steadying fingers taught their
    infant steps to frame,
'Twas thy loving gentle accents taught their lips to
    lisp each name,

As thine own they grew and blossomed, dear to
    thee they yet remain,
Take them back unto thy bosom, be a father once
    again!

UDYOGA

Unto thee, O Dhrita-rashtra! Pandu's sons in
 homage bend,
And a loving peaceful message through my willing
 lips they send:

Tell our monarch, more than father, by his sacred
 stern command
We have lived in pathless jungle, wandered far
 from land to land,

True unto our plighted promise, for we ever felt
 and knew,
To his promise Dhrita-rashtra cannot, will not be
 untrue!

Years of anxious toil are over and of woe and
 bitterness,
Years of waiting and of watching, years of danger
 and distress.

Like a dark unending midnight hung on us this
 age forlorn,
Streaks of hope and dawning brightness usher now
 the radiant morn!

Be unto us as a father, loving not inspired by
 wrath,

Be unto us as a teacher, pointing us the righteous path,

If perchance astray we wander, thy strong arm shall lead aright,
If our feeble bosom fainteth, help us with a father's might!

This, O king! the soft entreaty Pandu's sons to thee have made,
These are words the sons of Pandu unto Kuru's king have said,

Take their love, O gracious monarch! Let thy closing days be fair,
Let Duryodhan keep his kingdom, let the Pandavs have their share.

Call to mind their noble suffering, for the tale is dark and long,
Of the outrage they have suffered, of the insult and the wrong,

Exiled into Varnavata, destined unto death by flame,
For the gods assist the righteous, they with added prowess came,

UDYOGA

Exiled into Indra-prastha, by their toil and by their
  might
Cleared a forest, built a city, did the *rajasuya* rite,

Cheated of their realm and empire and of all they
  called their own,
In the jungle they have wandered and in Matsya
  lived unknown,

Once more quelling every evil they are stout of
  heart and hand,
Now redeem thy plighted promise and restore
  their throne and land!

*Trust me, mighty Dhrita-rashtra! trust me, lords who
  grace this hall,*
*Krishna pleads for peace and virtue, blessings unto you
  and all,*

*Slaughter not the arméd nations, slaughter not thy kith
  and kin,*
*Mark not, king, thy closing winters with the bloody
  stain of sin,*

*Let thy sons and Pandu's children stand beside thy
  ancient throne,*

*Cherish peace and cherish virtue, for thy days are
    almost done!"*

VI
BHISHMA'S SPEECH

From the monarch's ancient bosom sighs and sobs
    convulsive broke,
Bhishma wiped his manly eyelids and to proud
    Duryodhan spoke:

"Listen, prince, for righteous Krishna counsels
    love and holy peace,
Listen, youth, and may thy fortune with thy
    passing years increase!

Yield to Krishna's words of wisdom, for thy weal
    he nobly strives,
Yield and save thy friends and kinsmen, save thy
    cherished subjects' lives,

Foremost race in all this wide earth is Hastina's
    royal line,
Bring not on them dire destruction by a sinful act
    of thine!

Sons and fathers, friends and brothers, shall in
  mutual conflict die,
Kinsmen slain by dearest kinsmen shall upon the
  red field lie,

Hearken unto Krishna's counsel, unto wise
  Vidura's word,
Be thy mother's fond entreaty and thy father's
  mandate heard!

Tempt not wrath and fiery vengeance on thy old
  heroic race,
Tread not in the path of darkness, seek the path of
  light and grace,

Listen to thy king and father, he hath Kuru's
  empire graced,
Listen to thy queen and mother, she hath nursed
  thee on her breast!"

VII
DRONA'S SPEECH

Out spake Drona priest and warrior, and his words
  were few and high,

THE MAHABHARATA

Clouded was Duryodhan's forehed, wrathful was
    Duryodhan's eye:

"Thou hast heard the holy counsel which the
    righteous Krishna said,
Ancient Bhishma's voice of warning thou hast in
    thy bosom weighed,

Peerless in their godlike wisdom are these chiefs in
    peace or strife,
Truest friends to thee, Duryodhan, pure and
    sinless in their life!

Take their counsel, and thy kinsmen fasten in the
    bonds of peace,
May the empire of the Kurus and their warlike
    fame increase,

List unto thy old preceptor! Faithless is thy
    fitful star,
And they feed thy passions falsely, those who urge
    and counsel war!

Crownéd kings and arméd nations will contest for
    thee in vain,
Vainly brothers, sons, and kinsmen will for thee
    their lifeblood drain,

For the victor's crown and glory never, never can
   be thine,
Krishna conquers, and brave Arjun! mark these
   deathless words of mine!

I have trained the youthful Arjun, seen him bend
   the warlike bow,
Marked him charge the hostile forces, marked him
   smite the scattered foe.

Fiery son of Jamadagni owned no greater loftier
   might,
Breathes on earth no mortal warrior conquers
   Arjun in the fight!

Krishna too, in war resistless, comes from
   Dwarka's distant shore,
And the bright-gods quake before him whom the
   fair Devaki bore,

These are foes thou may'st not conquer, take an
   ancient warrior's word,
Act thou as thy heart decideth, thou art Kuru's
   king and lord!"

VIII
VIDURA'S SPEECH

Then in gentler voice Vidura sought his pensive
    mind to tell,
From his lips serene and softly words of woe and
    anguish fell:

"Not for thee I grieve, Duryodhan, slain by
    vengeance fierce and keen,
For thy father weeps my bosom and the aged Kuru
    queen!

Sons and grandsons, friends and kinsmen
    slaughtered in this fatal war,
Homeless, cheerless, on this wide earth they shall
    wander long and far,

Friendless, kinless, on this wide earth whither shall
    they turn and fly,
Like some birds bereft of plumage, they shall pine
    awhile and die,

Of their race and sad survivors they shall wander
    o'er the earth,

Curse the fatal day, Duryodhan, saw thy sad and
   woeful birth!"

IX
DHRITA-RASHTRA'S SPEECH

Tear-drops filled his sightless eyeballs, anguish
   shook his agéd frame,
As the monarch soothed Duryodhan by each fond
   endearing name:

"Listen, dearest son, Duryodhan, shun this dark
   and fatal strife,
Cast not grief and death's black shadows on thy
   parents' closing life,

Krishna's heart is pure and spotless, true and wise
   the words he said,
We may win a worldwide empire with the noble
   Krishna's aid,

Seek the friendship of Yudhishthir loved of
   righteous gods above,
And unite the scattered Kurus by the lasting tie
   of love!

Now at full is tide of fortune, never may it come
   again,
Strive and win, or ever after all repentance may
   be vain.

Peace is righteous Krishna's counsel and he comes
   to offer peace,
Take the offered boon, Duryodhan! Let all strife
   and hatred cease!"

X

DURYODHAN'S SPEECH

Silent sat the proud Duryodhan wrathful in the
   council hall,
Spake to mighty-arméd Krishna and to Kuru
   warriors all:

"Ill becomes thee, Dwarka's chieftain, in the paths
   of sin to move,
Bear for me a secret hatred, for the Pandavs
   secret love,

And my father, wise Vidura, ancient Bhishma,
   Drona bold,

UDYOGA

Join thee in this bitter hatred, turn on me their
    glances cold!

What great crime or darkening sorrow shadows
    o'er my bitter fate,
That ye chiefs and Kuru's monarch mark
    Duryodhan for your hate,

Speak, what nameless guilt or folly, secret sin to
    me unknown,
Turns from me your sweet affection, father's love
    that was my own?

If Yudhishthir, fond of gambling, played a heedless
    reckless game,
Lost his empire and his freedom, was it then
    Duryodhan's blame,

And if freed from shame and bondage in his folly
    played again,
Lost again and went to exile, wherefore doth he
    now complain?

Weak are they in friends and forces, feeble is their
    fitful star,
Wherefore then in pride and folly seek with us
    unequal war,

Shall we, who to mighty INDRA scarce will do the
 homage due,
Bow to homeless sons of Pandu and their
 comrades faint and few,

Bow to them while warlike Drona leads us as in
 days of old,
Bhishma greater than the bright-gods, archer
 Karna true and bold?

If in dubious game of battle we should forfeit fame
 and life,
Heaven will ope its golden portals for the Kshatra
 slain in strife,

If unbending to our foemen we should press the
 gory plain,
Stingless is the bed of arrows, death for us will
 have no pain!

For the Kshatra knows no terror of his foeman in
 the field,
Breaks like hardened forest timber, bends not,
 knows not how to yield,

So the ancient sage Matanga of the warlike
 Kshatra said,

UDYOGA

Save to priest and sage preceptor unto none he
    bends his head!

Indra-prastha which my father weakly to
    Yudhishthir gave,
Nevermore shall go unto him while I live and
    brothers brave,

Kuru's undivided kingdom Dhrita-rashtra rules
    alone,
Let us sheathe our swords in friendship and the
    monarch's empire own,

If in past in thoughtless folly once the realm was
    broke in twain,
Kuru-land is re-united, never shall be split again!

*Take my message to my kinsmen, for Duryodhan's
    words are plain,*
Portion of the Kuru empire sons of Pandu seek in vain,

*Town nor village, mart nor hamlet, help us righteous
    gods in heaven,*
*Spot that needle's point can cover shall not unto
    them be given!"*

BOOK VIII
BHISHMA-BADHA
(Fall of Bhishma)

All negotiations for a peaceful partition of the Kuru kingdom having failed, both parties now prepared for a battle, perhaps the most sanguinary that was fought on the plains of India in the ancient times. It was a battle of nations, for all warlike races in Northern India took a share in it.

Duryodhan's army consisted of his own division, as well as the divisions of ten allied kings. Each allied power is said to have brought one *akshauhini* troops, and if we reduce this fabulous number to the moderate figure of ten thousand, including horse and foot, cars and elephants, Duryodhan's army including his own division was over a hundred thousand strong.

Yudhishthir had a smaller army, said to have been seven *akshauhinis* in number, which we may by a similar reduction reckon to be seventy thousand. His father-in-law the king of the Panchalas, and Arjun's relative the king of the Matsyas, were his principal allies. Krishna joined him as his friend and adviser, and as the charioteer of Arjun, but the Vrishnis as a nation had joined Duryodhan.

When the two armies were drawn up in array and faced each other, and Arjun saw his revered elders and dear friends and relations among his foes, he was unwilling to fight. It was on this occasion that Krishna explained to him the great principles of Duty in that memorable work called the *Bhagavat-gita* which has been translated into so many European languages. Belief in one Supreme Deity is the underlying thought of this work, and ever and anon, as Professor Garbe remarks, "does Krishna revert to the doctrine that for every man, no matter to what caste he may belong, the zealous performance of his duty and the discharge of his obligations is his most important work."

Duryodhan chose the grand old fighter Bhishma as the commander-in-chief of his army, and for ten days Bhishma held his own and inflicted serious loss on Yudhishthir's army. The principal incidents of these ten days, ending with the fall of Bhishma, are narrated in this Book.

This Book is an abridgment of Book vi. of the original text.

I
PANDAVS ROUTED BY BHISHMA

Ushas with her crimson fingers oped the portals of
   the day,
Nations armed for mortal combat in the field of
   battle lay,

Beat of drum and blare of trumpet and the
   sankha's lofty sound,
By the answering cloud repeated, shook the hills
   and tented ground,

And the voice of sounding weapons which the
   warlike archers drew,
And the neigh of battle chargers as the arméd
   horsemen flew,

Mingled with the rolling thunder of each swiftly-
   speeding car,
And with pealing bells proclaiming mighty
   elephants of war!

Bhishma led the Kuru forces, strong as Death's
   resistless flail,

Human chiefs nor bright Immortals could against
  his might prevail,

Helmet-wearing, gallant Arjun came in pride and
  mighty wrath,
Held aloft his famed *Gandiva*, strove to cross the
  chieftain's path!

Abhimanyu son of Arjun, whom the fair Subhadra
  bore,
Drove against Kosala's monarch famed in arms
  and holy lore,

Hurling down Kosala's standard he the dubious
  combat won,
Barely escaped with life the monarch from the
  fiery Arjun's son!

With his fated foe Duryodhan, Bhima strove in
  deathful war,
And against the proud Duhsasan brave Nakula
  drove his car,

Sahadeva mighty bowman, then the fierce
  Durmukha sought,
And the righteous king Yudhishthir with the car-
  borne Salya fought,

BHISHMA-BADHA

Ancient feud and deathless hatred fired the
  Brahman warrior bold,
Drona with the proud Panchalas fought once more
  his feud of old!

Nations from the Eastern regions 'gainst the bold
  Virata pressed,
Kripa met the wild Kaikeyas hailing from the
  furthest West,

Drupad proud and peerless monarch with his
  cohorts onward bore
'Gainst the warlike Jayadratha chief of Sindhu's
  sounding shore,

Chedis and the valiant Matsyas, nations gathered
  from afar,
Bhojas and the fierce Kambojas mingled in the
  dubious war!

Through the day the battle lasted, and no mortal
  tongue can tell
What unnumbered chieftains perished and what
  countless soldiers fell.

And the son knew not his father, and the sire knew
  not his son,

Brother fought against his brother, strange the
   deeds of valour done!

Horses fell, and shafts of chariots shivered in
   resistless shock,
Hurled against the foreman's chariots speeding
   like the rolling rock,

Elephants by *mahuts* driven furiously each
   other tore,
Trumpeting with trunks uplifted on the serried
   soldiers bore!

Ceaseless plied the gallant troopers, with a stern
   unyielding might,
Pikes and axes, clubs and maces, swords and
   spears and lances bright,

Horsemen flew as forkéd lightning, heroes fought
   in shining mail,
Archers poured their feathered arrows like the
   bright and glistening hail!

Bhishma leader of the Kurus, as declined the
   dreadful day,
Through the shattered Pandav legions forced his
   all-resistless way,

BHISHMA-BADHA

Onward went his palm-tree standard through the
 hostile ranks of war,
Matsyas, Kasis, nor Panchalas faced the mighty
 Bhishma's car!

But the fiery son of Arjun, filled with shame and
 bitter wrath,
Turned his car and tawny coursers to obstruct the
 chieftain's path,

Vainly fought the youthful warrior though his darts
 were pointed well,
And dissevered from his chariot Bhishma's palm-
 tree standard fell,

Anger stirred the ancient Bhishma and he rose in
 all his might,
Abhimanyu pierced with arrows fell and fainted in
 the fight!

Then to save the son of Arjun, Matsya's gallant
 princes came,
Brave Uttara, noble Sweta, youthful warriors
 known to fame,

Ah! too early fell the warriors in that sad and fatal
 strife,

Matsya's dames and dark-eyed maidens wept the
  princes' shortened life!

Slain by cruel fate untimely fell two brothers
  young and good,
Dauntless still the youngest brother, proud and
  gallant Sankha stood,

But the helmet-wearing Arjun came to stop the
  victor's path,
And to save the fearless Sankha from the ancient
  Bhishma's wrath,

Drupad too, Panchala's monarch, swiftly rushed
  into the fray,
Strove to shield the broken Pandavs and to stop
  the victor's way.

But as fire cousumes the forest, wrathful Bhishma
  slew the foe,
None could face his sounding chariot and his ever-
  circled bow,

And the fainting Pandav warriors marked the foe,
  resistless, bold,
Shook like unprotected cattle tethered in the
  blighting cold!

BHISHMA-BADHA

Onward came the mighty Bhishma and the
    slaughter fiercer grew,
From his bow like hissing serpents still the
    glistening arrows flew,

Onward came the ancient warrior and his path was
    strewn with dead,
And the broken Pandav forces, crushed and
    driven, scattered fled,

Friendly night and gathering darkness closed the
    slaughter of the day,
To their tents the sons of Pandu held their sad and
    weary way!

II

KURUS ROUTED BY ARJUN

Grieved at heart the good Yudhishthir wept the
    losses of the day,
Sought the aid of gallant Krishna for the
    morning's fresh array,

And when from the eastern mountains SURYA
    drove his fiery car,

THE MAHABHARATA

Krishna and the helmèd Arjun strove to turn the
  tide of war.

Bhishma's glorious palm-tree standard o'er the
  field of battle rose,
Arjun's monkey-standard glittered cleaving
  through the serried foes,

Devas from their cloud-borne chariots, and
  Gandharvas from the sky,
Gazed in mute and speechless wonder on the
  human chiefs from high!

While with dauntless valour Arjun still the mighty
  Bhishma sought,
Warlike prince of fair Panchala with the doughty
  Drona fought,

Ceaseless 'gainst the proud preceptor sent his
  darts like summer rain,
Baffled by the skill of Drona, Dhrista-dyumna
  strove in vain!

But the fiercer darts of Drona pierced the prince's
  shattered mail,
Hurtling on his battle chariot like an angry shower
  of hail,

BHISHMA-BADHA

And they rent in twain his bowstring and they cut
 his pond'rous mace,
Slew his steeds and chariot-driver, streaked with
 blood his godlike face.

Dauntless still Panchala's hero, springing from his
 shattered car,
Like a hungry desert lion with his sabre rushed
 to war,

Dashed aside the darts of Drona with his broad
 and ample shield,
With his sabre brightly flaming fearless trod the
 reddened field!

In his fury and his rashness he had fallen on
 that day,
But the ever-watchful Bhima stopped the proud
 preceptor's way,

Proud Duryodhan marked with anger Bhima
 rushing in his car,
And he sent Kalinga's forces to the thickening
 ranks of war.

Onward came Kalinga's forces with the dark
 tornado's might,

THE MAHABHARATA

Dusky chiefs, Nishada warriors, gloomy as the
 sable night,

Rose the shout of warring nations surging to the
 battle's fore,
Like the angry voice of tempest and the ocean's
 troubled roar,

And like darkly rolling breakers ranks of serried
 warriors flew,
Scarcely in the thickening darkness friends and kin
 from foemen knew!

Fell the young prince of Kalinga by the wrathful
 Bhima slain,
But against Kalinga's monarch baffled Bhima
 fought in vain,

Safely sat the eastern monarch on his *howda's*
 lofty seat,
Till upon the giant tusker Bhima sprang with
 agile feet,

Then he struck with fatal fury, brave Kalinga fell
 in twain,
Scattered fled his countless forces when they saw
 their leader slain!

BHISHMA-BADHA

Darkly rolled the tide of battle where Duryodhan's
  valiant son
Strove against the son of Arjun famed for deeds of
  valour done,

Proud Duryodhan marked the contest with a
  father's anxious heart,
Came to save his gallant Lakshman from brave
  Abhimanyu's dart,

And the helmet-wearing Arjun marked his son
  among his foes,
Wheeled from far his battle-chariot and in wrath
  terrific rose!

"Arjun!" "Arjun!" cried the Kurus, and in panic
  broke and fled,
Steed and tusker turned from battle, soldiers fell
  among the dead,

Godlike Krishna drove the coursers of resistless
  Arjun's car,
And the sound of Arjun's *sankha* rose above the
  cry of war,

And the voice of his *Gandiva* spread a terror far
  and near,

Crushed and broken, faint and frightened, fled the
>   Kurus in their fear,

Onward still through scattered foemen conquering
>   Arjun held his way,
Till the evening's gathering darkness closed the
>   action of the day!

III

BHISHMA AND ARJUN MEET

Anxious was the proud Duryodhan when the
>   golden morning came,
For before the car of Arjun fled each Kurn chief
>   of fame,

Brave Duryodhan shook in anger and a tremor
>   moved his frame,
As he spake to ancient Bhishma words of wrath in
>   bitter shame:

"Bhishma! dost thou lead the Kurus in this battle's
>   crimson field,
Warlike Drona, doth he guard us like a broad and
>   ample shield?

BHISHMA-BADHA

Wherefore then before yon Arjun do the valiant
    Kurus fly,
Wherefore doth our leader linger when he hears
    the battle cry?

Doth a secret love for Pandavs quell our leader's
    matchless might,
With a halting zeal for Kurus doth the noble
    Bhishma fight?

Pardon, chief, if for the Pandavs doth thy partial
    heart incline,
Yield thy place, let faithful Karna lead my gallant
    Kuru line!"

Anger flamed on Bhishma's forehead and the tear
    was in his eye,
And in accents few and trembling thus the warrior
    made reply:

"Vain our toil, unwise Duryodhan! Nor can
    Bhishma warrior old,
Nor can Drona skilled in weapons, Karna archer
    proud and bold,

Wash the stain of deeds unholy and of wrongs and
    outraged laws,

Conquer with a load of cunning 'gainst a right and righteous cause,

Deaf to wisdom's voice, Duryodhan, deaf to parents and to kin,
Thou shalt perish in thy folly, in thy unrepented sin!

For the wrongs and insults offered unto good Yudhishthir's wife,
For the kingdom from him stolen, for the plots against his life,

For the dreadful oath of Bhima, for the holy counsel given,
Vainly given by saintly Krishna, thou art doomed by righteous Heaven!

Meanwhile since he leads thy forces, Bhishma still shall meet his foe,
Or to conquer or to perish to the battle's front I go."

Speaking thus, unto the battle ancient Bhishma held his way,
Sweeping all before his chariot as he swept them day by day,

BHISHMA-BADHA

And the army of Yudhishthir shook from end to
 farthest end,
Arjun nor the valiant Krishna could against the
 tide contend!

Cars were shattered, fled the coursers, elephants
 were pierced and slain,
Shafts of chariots, broken standards, lifeless
 soldiers strewed the plain,

Coats of mail were left by warriors as they ran with
 streaming hair,
Soldiers fled like herds of cattle stricken by a
 sudden fear!

Krishna, Arjun's chariot-driver, and a chief of
 righteous fame,
Marked the broken Pandav forces, spake in grief
 and bitter shame:

"Arjun! not in hour of battle hath it been they
 wont to fly,
Forward lay thy path of glory, or to conquer or
 to die!

If to-day with angry Bhishma, Arjun shuns the
 dubious fight,

Shame on Krishna! if he joins thee in this sad
  inglorious flight,

Be it mine alone, O Arjun! warrior's wonted work
  to know,
Krishna with his fiery discus smites the all-
  resistless foe!"

Then he flung the reins to Arjun, left the steeds
  and sounding car,
Leaped upon the field of battle, rushed into the
  dreadful war,

"Shame!" cried Arjun in his anger, "Krishna shall
  not wage the fight,
Nor shall Arjun like a recreant seek for safety in his
  flight!"

And he dashed behind the warrior and on foot the
  chief pursued,
Caught him as the angry Krishna still his distant
  foeman viewed,

Stalwart Arjun lifted Krishna, as the storm lifts up
  a tree,
Placed him on his battle-chariot and he bent to
  him his knee:

BHISHMA-BADHA

"Pardon, Krishna, this compulsion, pardon this
    transgression bold,
But while Arjun lives, O chieftain! weapon of thy
    wrath withhold!

By my warlike Abhimanyu, fair Subhadra's
    darling boy,
By my brothers, dearer, truer, than in hours of
    pride and joy,

By my troth I pledge thee, Krishna,—let thy angry
    discus sleep,—
Archer Arjun meets his foeman, and his plighted
    word will keep."

Forthwith rushed the fiery Arjun in his sounding
    battle-car,
And like waves before him parted serried ranks of
    hostile war,

Vainly hurled his lance Duryodhan 'gainst the
    valiant warrior's face,
Vainly Salya, king of Madra, threw with skill his
    pond'rous mace,

With disdain the godlike Arjun dashed the feeble
    darts aside,

Held aloft his famed *Gandiva* as he stood with haughty pride,

Beat of drum and blare of *sankha* and the thunder of his car,
And his weapon's fearful accents rose terrific near and far!

Came resistless Pandav forces, sweeping onward wave on wave,
Chedis, Matsyas, and Panchalas, chieftains true and warriors brave,

Onward too came forth the Kurus by the matchless Bhishma led,
Shouts arose and cry of anguish midst the dying and the dead,

But the evening closed in darkness and the night-fires fitful flared,
Fainting troops and bleeding chieftains to their various tents repaired!

IV
DURYODHAN'S EIGHT BROTHERS SLAIN

Dawned another day of battle; Kurus knew that
>   day too well,
Widowed queens of fair Hastina wept before the
>   evening fell,

For as whirlwind of destruction Bhima swept in
>   mighty wrath,
Broke the serried line of tuskers vainly sent to
>   cross his path,

Smote Duryodhan with his arrows, three terrific
>   darts and five,
Smote proud Salya; from the battle scarce they
>   bore the chiefs alive!

Then Duryodhan's fourteen brothers rushed into
>   the dreadful fray,
Fatal was the luckless moment, inauspicious was
>   the day,

Licked his mouth the vengeful Bhima, and he
>   shook his bow and lance,

As the lion lolls his red tongue when he see his
    prey advance,

Short and fierce the furious combat; six pale
    princes turned and fled,
Eight of proud Duryodhan's brothers fell and
    slumbered with the dead!

V

SATYAKI'S SONS SLAIN

Morning with her fiery radiance oped the portals
    of the day,
Shone once more on Kuru warriors, Pandav chiefs
    in dread array,

Bhima and the gallant Arjun led once more the
    van of war,
But the proud preceptor Drona faced them in his
    sounding car!

Still with gallant son of Arjun, Lakshman strove
    with bow and shield,
Vainly strove; his faithful henchman bore him
    bleeding from the field,

BHISHMA-BADHA

Lakshman son of proud Duryodhan, Abhimanyu Arjun's son,

Doomed to die in youth and glory 'neath the same revolving sun!

Sad the day for Vrishni warriors! Brave Satyaki's sons of might

'Gainst the cruel Bhuri-sravas strove in unrelenting fight,

Ten brave brothers, pride of Vrishni, fell upon that fatal day,

Slain by mighty Bhuri-sravas on the battle's red field lay!

VI
BHIMA'S DANGER AND RESCUE

Dawned another day of slaughter; heedless Bhima forced his way

Through Duryodhan's serried legions, where dark death and danger lay,

And a hundred foemen gathered and unequal was the strife,

Bhima strove with furious valour, for his forfeit
  was his life!

Fair Panchala's watchful monarch saw the danger
  from afar,
Forced his way where bleeding Bhima fought
  beside his shattered car,

And he helped the fainting warrior, placed him on
  his chariot-seat,
But the Kurus darkly gathered, surging round as
  waters meet!

Arjun's son and twelve brave chieftains dashed
  into the dubious fray,
Rescued Bhima and proud Drupad from the
  Kurus' grim array,

Surging still the Kuru forces onward came with
  ceaseless might,
Drona smote the scattered Pandavs till the
  darksome hours of night!

VII
PANDAVS ROUTED BY BHISHAMA

Morning came and angry Arjun rushed into the
 dreadful war,
Krishna drove his milk-white coursers, onward
 flew his sounding car,

And before his monkey banner quailed the faint
 and frightened foes,
Till like star on billowy ocean Bhishma's palm-tree
 banner rose!

Vainly then the good Yudhishthir, stalwart Bhima,
 Arjun brave,
Strove with useless toil and valour shattered ranks
 of war to save,

Vainly too the Pandav brothers on the peerless
 Bhishma fell,
Gods in sky nor earthly warriors Bhishma's
 matchless might could quell!

Fell Yudhishthir's lofty standard, shook his chariot
 battle-tost,

Fell his proud and fiery coursers, and the dreadful day was lost,

Sahadeva and Nakula vainly strove with all their might,
Till their broken scattered forces rested in the shades of night!

VIII

IRAVAT SLAIN

Morning saw the turn of battle; Bhishma's charioteer was slain,
And his coursers uncontrolléd flew across the reddened plain,

Ill it fared with Kuru forces when their leader went astray,
And their foremost chiefs and warriors with the dead and dying lay.

But Gandhara's mounted princes rode across the battle-ground,—
For its steeds and matchless chargers is Gandhara's realm renowned,

BHISHMA-BADHA

And to smite the young Iravat fierce Gandhara's
    princes swore,—
Brave Iravat son of Arjun, whom a Naga princess
    bore!

Mounted on their milk-white chargers proudly did
    the princes sweep,
Like the sea-birds skimming gaily o'er the bosom
    of the deep,

Five of stout Gandhara's princes in that fatal
    combat fell,
And a sixth in fear and faintness fled the woeful
    tale to tell!

Short, alas, Iravat's triumph, transient was the
    victor's joy,
Alumbusha dark and dreadful came against the
    gallant boy,

Fierce and fateful was the combat, mournful is the
    tale to tell,
Like a lotus rudely severed gallant son of
    Arjun fell!

Arjun heard the tale of sorrow and his heart was
    filled with grief,

THE MAHABHARATA

And he spake a father's anguish in his accents few
   and brief:

"Wherefore, Krishna, for a kingdom mingle in this
   fatal fray,
Kinsmen killed and comrades slaughtered,—dear,
   alas, the price we pay!

Woe unto Hastina's empire built upon our
   children's grave,
Dearer than the throne of monarchs was Iravat
   young and brave,

Young in years and rich in beauty, with thy
   mother's winsome eye,
Art thou slain, my gallant warrior, and thy father
   was not nigh?

But thy young blood calls for vengeance! Noble
   Krishna, drive the car,
Let them feel the father's prowess, those who slew
   the son in war!"

And he dashed the rising tear-drop and his words
   were few and brief,
Broken ranks and slaughtered chieftains spoke an
   angry father's grief,

BHISHMA-BADHA

Bhima too revenged Iravat, and as onward still
    he flew,
Brothers of the proud Duryodhan in that fatal
    combat slew,

Still advanced the fatal carnage till the darksome
    close of day,
When the wounded and the weary with the dead
    and dying lay!

IX
PANDAVS ROUTED BY BHISHMA

Fell the thickening shades of darkness of the red
    and ghastly plain,
Torches by the white tents flickered, red fires
    showed the countless slain,

With a bosom sorrow-laden proud Duryodhan
    drew his breath,
Wept the issue of the battle and his warlike
    brother's death.

Spent with grief and silent sorrow slow the Kuru
    monarch went

Where arose in dewy starlight Bhishma's proud
  and snowy tent,

And with tears and soft entreaty thus the sad
  Duryodhan spoke,
And his mournful bitter accents oft by heaving
  sighs were broke:

"Bhishma! on thy matchless prowess Kuru's hopes
  and fates depend,
Gods nor men with warlike Bhishma can in field of
  war contend,

Brave in war are sons of Pandu, but they face not
  Bhishma's might,
In their fierce and deathless hatred slay my
  brothers in the fight!

Mind thy pledge, O chief of Kurus, save Hastina's
  royal race,
On the ancient king my father grant thy never-
  failing grace,

If within thy noble bosom,—pardon cruel words
  I say,—
Secret love for sons of Pandu holds a soft and
  partial sway,

BHISHMA-BADHA

If thy inner heart's affection unto Pandu's sons
    incline,
Grant that Karna lead my forces 'gainst the
    foeman's hostile line!"

Bhishma's heart was full of sadness and his eyelids
    dropped a tear,
Soft and mournful were his accents and his vision
    true and clear:

"Vain, Duryodhan, is this contest, and thy mighty
    host is vain,
Why with blood of friendly nations drench this red
    and reeking plain?

They must win who, strong in virtue, fight for
    virtue's stainless laws,
Doubly armed the stalwart warrior who is armed
    in righteous cause,

Think, Duryodhan, when *Gandharvas* took thee
    captive and a slave,
Did not Arjun rend thy fetters, Arjun righteous
    chief and brave,

When in Matsya's fields of pasture captured we
    Virata's kine,

Did not Arjun in his valour best thy countless
   force and mine?

Krishna now hath come to Arjun, Krishna drives
   his battle-car,
Gods nor men can face these heroes in the field of
   righteous war,

Ruin frowns on thee, Duryodhan, and upon thy
   impious State,
In thy pride and in thy folly thou hast courted
   cruel fate,

Bhishma still will do his duty, and his end it is
   not far,
Then may other chieftains follow,—fatal is this
   Kuru war!"

Dawned a day of mighty slaughter and of dread
   and deathful war,
Ancient Bhishma in his anger drove once more his
   sounding car,

Morn to noon and noon to evening none could
   face the victor's wrath,
Broke and shattered, faint and frightened, Pandavs
   fled before his path,

Still amidst the dead and dying moved his proud
    resistless car,
Till the gathering night and darkness closed the
    horrors of the war!

X
FALL OF BHISHMA

Good Yudhishthir gazed with sorrow on the dark
    and ghastly plain,
Shed his tears on chiefs and warriors by the
    matchless Bhishma slain:

"Vain this unavailing battle, vain this woeful loss
    of life,
'Gainst the death-compelling Bhishma hopeless in
    this arduous strife!

As a lordly tusker tramples on a marsh of feeble
    reeds,
As a forest conflagration on the parchéd woodland
    feeds,

Bhishma tramples on my forces in his mighty
    battle-car,

God nor mortal chief can face him in the gory
field of war!

Vain our toil and vain the valour of our kinsmen
loved and lost,
Vainly fight my faithful brothers by a luckless
fortune crost,

Nations pour their lifeblood vainly, ceaseless wakes
the sound of woe,
Krishna, stop this cruel carnage, unto woods once
more we go!"

Sad they held a midnight council and the chiefs in
silence met,
And they went to ancient Bhishma, love and mercy
to entreat,

Bhishma loved the sons of Pandu with a father's
loving heart,
But from troth unto Duryodhan righteous
Bhishma would not part!

"Sons of Pandu!" said the chieftain, "Prince
Duryodhan is my lord,
Bhishma is no faithless servant nor will break his
plighted word,

BHISHMA-BADHA

Valiant are ye, noble princes, but the chief is yet unborn,
While I lead the course of battle, who the tide of war can turn!

Listen more. With vanquished foeman, or who falls or takes to fight,
Casts his weapons, craves for mercy, ancient Bhishma doth not fight,

Bhishma doth not fight a rival who submits, fatigued and worn,
Bhishma doth not fight the wounded, doth not fight a woman born!"

Back unto their tents the Pandavs turn with Krishna deep and wise,
He unto the anxious Arjun thus in solemn whisper cries:

"Arjun, there is hope of triumph! Hath not truthful Bhishma sworn
He will fight no wounded warrior, he will fight no woman born?

Female child was brave Sikhandin, Drupad's youngest son of pride,

Gods have turned him to a warrior, placed him by Yudhishthir's side,

Place him in the van of battle, mighty Bhishma leaves the strife,
Then with ease we fight and conquer, and the forfeit is his life!"

"Shame!" exclaimed the angry Arjun, "not in secret heroes fight,
Not behind a child or woman screen their valour and their might,

Krishna, loth is archer Arjun to pursue this hateful strife,
Trick against the sinless Bhishma, fraud upon his spotless life!

Listen, good and noble Krishna; as a child I climbed his knee,
As a boy I called him father, hung upon him lovingly,

Perish conquest dearly purchased by a mean deceitful strife,
Perish crown and jeweled scepter won with Bhishma's saintly life!"

BHISHMA-BADHA

Gravely answered noble Krishna: "Bhishma falls
by close of day,
Victim to the cause of virtue, he himself hath
showed the way,

Dear or hated be the foeman, Arjun, thou shalt
fight and slay,
Wherefore else the blood of nations hast thou
poured from day to day?"

Morning dawned, and mighty Arjun, Abhimanyu
young and bold,
Drupad monarch of Panchala, and Virata stern
and old,

Brave Yudhishthir and his brothers clad in arms
and shining mail,
Rushed to war where Bhishma's standard gleamed
and glittered in the gale!

Proud Duryodhan marked their onset and its fatal
purpose knew,
And his bravest men and chieftains 'gainst the
fiery Pandavs threw,

With Kamboja's stalwart monarch and with
Drona's mighty son,

With the valiant bowman Kripa stemmed the
  battle still unwon!

And his younger, fierce Duhsasan, thirsting for the
  deathful war,
'Gainst the helmet-wearing Arjun drew his mighty
  battle-car,

As the high and rugged mountain meets the angry
  ocean's sway,
Proud Duhsasan warred with Arjun in his wild and
  onward way,

And as myriad white-winged sea-birds swoop
  upon the darksome wave,
Clouds of darts and glistening lances drank the red
  blood of the brave!

Other warlike Kuru chieftains came, the bravest
  and the best,
Drona's self and Bhagadatta monarch of the
  farthest East,

Car-borne Salya mighty warrior, king of Madra's
  distant land,
Princes from Avanti's regions, chiefs from Malwa's
  rocky strand,

BHISHMA-BADHA

Jayadratha matchless fighter, king of Sindhu's
sounding shore,
Chitrasena and Vikarna, countless chiefs and
warriors more!

And they faced the fiery Pandavs peerless in their
warlike might,
Long and dreadful raged the combat, darkly
closed the dubious fight,

Dust arose like clouds of summer, glistening darts
like lightning played,
Darksome grew the sky with arrows, thicker grew
the gloomy shade,

Cars went down and mailéd horsemen, soldiers
fell in dread array,
Elephants with white tusks broken and with
mangled bodies lay!

Arjun and the stalwart Bhima piercing through
their countless foes,
Side by side impelled their chariots where the
palm-tree standard rose,

Where the peerless ancient Bhishma on that dark
and fatal day,

Warring with the banded nations still resistless
    held his way!

On he came, his palm-tree standard still the front
    of battle knew,
And like sun from dark clouds parting Bhishma
    burst on Arjun's view,

And his eyes brave Arjun shaded at the awe-
    inspiring sight,
Half he wished to turn for shelter from that chief
    of godlike might!

But bold Krishna drove his chariot, whispered low
    his fatal plan,
Arjun placed the young Sikhandin in the deathful
    battle's van,

Bhishma viewed the Pandav forces with a calm
    unmoving face,
Saw not Arjun's fair *Gandiva,* saw not Bhima's
    mighty mace,

Smiled to see the young Sikhandin rushing to the
    battle's fore,
Like the foam upon the billow when the mighty
    storm-winds roar!

BHISHMA-BADHA

Bhishma thought of word he plighted and of oath
    that he had sworn,
Dropped his arms before the warrior who a female
    child was born,

And the standard which no warrior ever saw in
    base retreat,
Idly stood upon the chariot, threw its shade on
    Bhishma's seat,

And the flagstaff fell dissevered on the crushed
    and broken car,
As from azure sky of midnight falls the meteor's
    flaming star!

Not Sikhandin's feeble arrows did the palm-tree
    standard fell,
Not Sikhandin's feeble lances did the peerless
    Bhishma quell,

True to oath and unresisting, Bhishma turned his
    face away,
Turned and fell; the sun declining marked the
    closing of the day!

Ended thus the fatal battle, truce came with the
    close of day,

Kurus and the silent Pandavs went where Bhishma
dying lay,

Arjun wept as for a father weeps a sad and
sorrowing son,
Good Yudhishthir cursed the morning Kuru-
kshetra's war begun,

Stood Duryodhan and his brothers mantled in the
gloom of grief,
Foes like loving brothers sorrowed round the great
the dying chief!

Arjun's keen and pointed arrows made the hero's
dying bed,
And in soft and gentle accents to Duryodhan thus
he said:

"List unto my words, Duryodhan, uttered with my
latest breath,
List to Bhishma's dying counsel and revere the
voice of death,

End this dread and deathful battle if thy stony
heart can grieve,
Save the chieftains doomed to slaughter, bid the
fated nations live,

BHISHMA-BADHA

Grant his kingdom to Yudhishthir righteous man
   beloved of Heaven,
Keep thy own Hastina's regions, be the hapless
   past forgiven!"

Vain, alas, the voice of Bhishma like the voice of
   angel spoke,
Hatred dearer than his lifeblood in the proud
   Duryodhan woke!

Darker grew the gloomy midnight and the princes
   went their way,
On his bed of pointed arrows Bhishma lone and
   dying lay,

Karna, though he loved not Bhishma whilst the
   chieftain lived in fame,
Gently to the dying Bhishma in the midnight
   darkness came!

Bhishma heard the tread of Karna and he oped his
   glazing eye,
Spake in love and spake in sadness and his bosom
   heaved a sigh:

"Pride and envy, noble Karna, filled our warlike
   hearts with strife,

Discord ends with breath departing, envy sinks
    with fleeting life!

More I have to tell thee, Karna, but my parting
    breath may fail,
Feeble are my dying accents and my parchéd lips
    are pale,

Arjun beats not noble Karna in the deeds of
    valour done,
Nor excels in birth and lineage, Karna, thou art
    Pritha's son!

Pritha bore thee, still unwedded, and the Sun
    inspired thy birth,
God-born man! No mightier archer treads this
    broad and spacious earth,

Pritha cast thee in her sorrow, hid thee with a
    maiden's shame,
And a driver, not thy father, nursed thee, chief of
    warlike fame,

Arjun is thy brother, Karna, end this sad
    fraternal war,
Seek not lifeblood of thy brother nor against him
    drive thy car!"

BHISHMA-BADHA

Vain, alas, the voice of Bhishma like the voice of
 angel spoke,
Hatred dearer than his lifeblood in the vengeful
 Karna woke!

Book IX
Drona-Badha
(Fall of Drona)

On the fall of Bhishma the Brahman chief Drona, preceptor of the Kuru and Pandav princes, was appointed the leader of the Kuru forces. For five days Drona held his own against the Pandavs, and some of the incidents of these days, like the fall of Abhimanyu and the vengeance of Arjun, are among the most stirring passages in the Epic. The description of the different standards of the Pandav and the Kuru warriors is also interesting. At last Drona slew his ancient foe the king of the Panchalas, and was then slain by his son the prince of the Panchalas.

The Book is an abridgment of Book vii. of the original text.

I
SINGLE COMBAT BETWEEN BHIMA AND SALYA

Morning ushered in the battle; Pandav warriors
 heard with dread
Drona priest and proud preceptor now the Kuru
 forces led,

And the foe-compelling Drona pledged his troth
 and solemn word,
He would take Yudhishthir captive to Hastina's
 haughty lord!

But the ever faithful Arjun to his virtuous elder
 bowed,
And in clear and manful accents spake his warlike
 thoughts aloud:

"Sacred is our great preceptor, sacred is
 acharya's life,
Arjun may not slay his teacher even in this mortal
 strife!

Saving this, command, O monarch, Arjun's bow
 and warlike sword,

DRONA-BADHA

For thy safety, honoured elder, Arjun stakes his
  plighted word,

Matchless in the art of battle is our teacher fierce
  and dread,
But he comes not to Yudhishthir save o'er blood of
  Arjun shed!"

Morning witnessed doughty Drona foremost in
  the battle's tide,
But Yudhishthir's warlike chieftains compassed
  him on every side,

Foremost of the youthful chieftains came resistless
  Arjun's son,—
Father's blood and milk of mothers fired his deeds
  of valour done!

As the lion of the jungle drags the ox into his lair,
Abhimanyu from his chariot dragged Paurava by
  the hair,

Jayadratha king of Sindhu marked the faint and
  captive chief,
Leaping from his car of battle wrathful came to his
  relief,

Abhimanyu left his captive, turned upon the
  mightier foe,
And with sword and hardened buckler gave and
  parried many a blow!

Rank to rank from both the forces cry of
  admiration rose,
Streaming men poured forth in wonder, watched
  the combat fierce and close,

Piercing Abhimanyu's buckler Jayadratha sent his
  stroke,
But the turned and twisted sword-blade snapping
  in the midway broke!

Weaponless the king of Sindhu ran into his
  sheltering car,
Salya came unto his rescue from a battle-field afar,

Dauntless, on the new assailant Arjun's son his
  weapon drew,
Interposing 'twixt the fighters Bhima's self on
  Salya flew!

Stoutest wrestlers in the armies, fiercest fighters
  with the mace,

DRONA-BADHA

Bhima and the stalwart Salya stood as rivals face
  to face,

Hempen fastening bound their maces and the wire
  of twisted gold,
Whirling bright in circling flashes, shook their staff
  the warriors bold!

Oft they struck, and sparks of red fire issued from
  the seasoned wood,
And like hornéd bulls infuriate Madra's king and
  Bhima stood,

Closer still they came like tigers closing with their
  reddened paws,
Or like tuskers with their red tusks, eagles with
  their rending claws!

Loud as INDRA'S peals of thunder still their blows
  were echoed round
Rank to rank the startled soldiers heard the oft-
  repeated sound,

But as strikes in vain the lightning on the solid
  mountain-rock,
Bhima nor the fearless Salya fell or moved beneath
  the shock!

Closer drew the watchful heroes and their clubs
   were wielded well,
Till by many blows belaboured both the fainting
   fighters fell,

Like a drunkard dazed and reeling Bhima rose his
   staff to wield,
Senseless Salya, heavy-breathing, henchman
   carried from the field,

Writhing like a wounded serpent, lifted from the
   field of war,
He was carried by his soldiers to the shelter of
   his car!

Drona still with matchless prowess strove to keep
   his plighted word,
Sought to take Yudhishthir captive to Duryodhan,
   Kuru's lord,

Vainly then the twin-born brothers came to cross
   the conqueror's path,
Matsya's lord, Panchala's monarch, vainly faced
   him in his wrath,

Rank to rank the cry resounded circling o'er the
   battle-field,

DRONA-BADHA

"Drona takes Yudhishthir captive with his bow and
    sword and shield!"

Arjun heard the dreadful message and in haste and
    fury came,
Strove to save his king and elder and redeem his
    loyal fame,

Speeding with his milk-white coursers dashed into
    the thick of war,
Blew his shrill and dreaded *sankha*, drove his
    sounding battle-car,

Fiercer, darker grew the battle, when above the
    reddened plain,
Evening drew her peaceful mantle o'er the living
    and the slain!

II

STANDARDS OF THE PANDAVS

Morning came; still round Yudhishthir Drona led
    the gathering war,
Arjun fought the Sam-saptakas in the battle-field
    afar,

But the prince of fair Panchala marked his father's ancient foe,
And against the doughty Drona, Dhrishta-dyumna bent his bow!

But as darksome cloudy masses angry gusts of storm divide,
Through the scattered fainting foemen Drona drove his car in pride,

Steeds went down and riven chariots, young Panchala turned and fled,
Onward drove resistless Drona o'er the dying and the dead!

One more prince of fair Panchala 'gainst the mighty Drona came,
Ancient feud ran in the red blood of Panchala's chiefs of fame,

Fated youth! with reckless valour still he fought his father's foe,
Fought and fell; relentless Drona laid the brave Satyajit low!

Surging still like ocean's billows other Pandav warriors came,

DRONA-BADHA

To protect their virtuous monarch and redeem
 their ancient fame,

Came in various battle-chariots drawn by steeds of
 every hue,
Various were the chieftains' standards which the
 warring nations knew!

Bhima drove his stalwart horses tinted like the
 dappled deer,
Grey and pigeon-coloured coursers bore
 Panchala's prince and peer,

Horses bred in famed Kamboja, dark and grey of
 deepest hue,
Brave Nakula's sumptuous chariot in the deathful
 battle drew,

Piebald horses trained to battle did young
 Sahadeva rein,
Ivory-white Yudhishthir's coursers with their
 flowing ebon mane,

And by him with gold umbrella valiant monarch
 Drupad came,
Horses of a bright bay-colour carried Matsya's
 king of fame.

THE MAHABHARATA

Varied as their varied courses gallantly their
    standards rose,
With their wondrous strange devices, terror of
    their arméd foes,

Water-jar on tawny deerskin, such was Drona's
    sign of war,—
Drona as a tender infant rested in a water-jar,

Golden moon with stars surrounding was
    Yudhishthir's sign of yore,
Silver lion was the standard tiger-waisted
    Bhima bore,

Brave Nakula's sign was red deer with its back of
    burnished gold,
Silver swan with bells resounding Sahadeva's
    onset told,

Golden peacock rich-emblazoned was young
    Abhimanyu's joy,
Vulture shone on Ghatotkacha, Bhima's proud
    and gallant boy.

Now Duryodhan marked the foemen heaving like
    the rising tide,

DRONA-BADHA

And he faced the wrathful Bhima towering in his
    tameless pride.

Short the war; for proud Duryodhan wounded
    from the battle fled,
And his warriors from fair Anga rested with the
    countless dead!

Wild with anger Bhagadatta, monarch of the
    farthest East,
With his still unconquered forces on the valiant
    Bhima pressed,

Came from far the wrathful Arjun and the battle's
    front he sought,
Where by eastern foes surrounded still the stalwart
    Bhima fought!

Fated monarch from the mighty Brahma-putra's
    sounding shore,
Land of rising sun will hail him and his noble
    peers no more,

For his tusker pierced by arrows trumpeted his
    dying wail,
Like a red and flaming meteor gallant Bhagadatta
    fell!

Then with rising wrath and anguish Karna's noble
  bosom bled,—
Karna who had stayed from battle while his rival
  Bhishma led,

Ancient hate and jealous anger clouded Karna's
  warlike heart,
And while Bhishma led, all idly slumbered Karna's
  bow and dart,

Now he marked with warrior's anguish all his
  comrades fled afar,
And his foeman Arjun sweeping o'er the red field
  of the war!

Hatred like a tongue of red fire shot from Karna's
  flaming eye,
And he sprang to meet his foeman or to conquer
  or to die,

Fierce and dubious was the battle, answering
  clouds gave back the din,
Karna met his dearest foeman and, alas, his
  nearest kin!

Bhima and Panchala's warriors unto Arjun's
  rescue came,

DRONA-BADHA

Proud Duryodhan came to Karna, and fair
    Sindhu's king of fame,

Fiercely raged the gory combat, when the night its
    shadows threw,
Wounded men and blood-stained chieftains to
    their nightly tents withdrew!

III
ABHIMANYU'S DEATH

Fatal was the blood-red morning purpling o'er the
    angry east,
Fatal day for Abhimanyu, bravest warrior and
    the best,

Countless were the gallant chieftains like the sands
    beside the sea,
None with braver bosom battled, none with hands
    more stout and free!

Brief, alas, thy radiant summers, fair Subhadra's
    gallant boy,
Loved of Matsya's soft-eyed princess and her
    young heart's pride and joy,

Brief, alas, thy sunlit winters, light of war too early
 quenched,
Peerless son of peerless Arjun, in the blood of
 foemen drenched!

Drona on that fatal morning ranged his dreadful
 battle-line
In a circle darkly spreading where the chiefs with
 chiefs combine,

And the Pandavs looked despairing on the battle's
 dread array,
Vainly strove to force a passage, vainly sought their
 onward way!

Abhimanyu, young and fiery, dashed alone into
 the war,
Reckless through the shattered forces all resistless
 drove his car,

Elephants and crashing standards, neighing steeds
 and warriors slain
Fell before the furious hero as he made a ghastly
 lane!

Proud Duryodhan rushed to battle, strove to stop
 the turning tide,

DRONA-BADHA

And his stoutest truest warriors fought by proud
    Duryodhan's side,

Onward still went Abhimanyu, Kurus strove and
    fought in vain,
Backward reeled and fell Duryodhan and his
    bravest chiefs were slain!

Next came Salya car-borne monarch 'gainst the
    young resistless foe,
Urged his fiery battle-coursers, stretched his
    death-compelling bow,

Onward still went Abhimanyu, Salya strove and
    fought in vain,
And his warriors took him bleeding from the
    reddened battle-plain!

Next Duhsasan darkly lowering thundered with
    his bended bow,
Abhimanyu smiled to see him, kinsman and the
    dearest foe,

"Art thou he," said Abhimanyu, "known for cruel
    word and deed,
Impious in thy heart and purpose, base and
    ruthless in thy greed?

Didst thou with the false Sakuni win a realm by low device,
Win his kingdom from Yudhishthir by ignoble trick of dice,

Didst thou in the council chamber with your insults foul and keen
By her flowing raven tresses drag Yudhishthir's stainless queen,

Didst thou speak to warlike Bhima as thy serf and bounden slave,
Wrong my father righteous Arjun, peerless prince and warrior brave?

Welcome! I have sought thee often, wished to cross thy tainted path,
Welcome! Dearest of all victims to my nursed and cherished wrath,

Reap the meed of sin and insult, draw on earth thy latest breath,
For I owe to Queen Draupadi, impious prince, thy speedy death!"

Like a snake upon an ant-hill, on Duhsasan's wicked heart

DRONA-BADHA

Fell with hissing wrath and fury Abhimanyu's
  fiery dart,

From the loss of blood Duhsasan fainted on his
  battle-car,
Kuru chieftains bore him senseless from the
  blood-stained scene of war!

Next in gleaming arms accoutered came
  Duryodhan's gallant son,
Proud and warlike as his father, famed for deeds of
  valour done,

Young in years and rich in valour, for alas! he
  fought too well,
And before his weeping father proud and gallant
  Lakshman fell!

Onward still went Abhimanyu midst the dying and
  the dead,
Shook from rank to rank the Kurus and their
  shattered army fled,

Then the impious Jayadratha, king of Sindhu's
  sounding shore,
Came forth in unrighteous concert with six car-
  borne warriors more,

THE MAHABHARATA

Darkly closed the fatal circle with the gulfing
   surge's moan,
Dauntless with the seven brave chieftains
   Abhimanyu fought alone!

Fell, alas, his peacock standard and his car was
   broke in twain,
Bow and sabre rent and shattered and his faithful
   driver slain,

Heedless yet of death and danger, misty with the
   loss of blood,
Abhimanyu wiped his forehead, gazed where dark
   his foemen stood!

Then with wild despairing valour, flickering flame
   and closing life,
Mace in hand the heedless warrior rushed to end
   the mortal strife,

Rushed upon his startled foemen, Abhimanyu
   fought and fell,
And his deeds to distant ages bards and wand'ring
   minstrels tell!

Like a tusker of the forest by surrounding hunters
   slain,

DRONA-BADHA

Like a wood-consuming wildfire quenched upon
 the distant plain,

Like a mountain-shaking tempest spent in force
 and hushed and still,
Like the red resplendent day-god setting on the
 western hill,

Like the moon serene and beauteous quenched in
 eclipse dark and pale,
Lifeless slumbered Abhimanyu when the softened
 starlight fell!

Done the day of death and slaughter, darkening
 shadows close around,
Wearied warriors seek for shelter on the vast and
 tented ground,

Soldiers' camp-fires brightly blazing, tent-lights
 shining from afar,
Cast their fitful gleam and radiance on the carnage
 of the war!

Arjun from a field at distance, where upon that
 day he fought,
With the ever faithful Krishna now his nightly
 shelter sought,

"Wherefore, Krishna," uttered Arjun, "evil omens
    strike my eye,
Thoughts of sadness fill my bosom, wake the long-
    forgotten sigh,

Wherefore voice of evening bugle speaks not on
    the battle-field,
Merry conch nor sounding trumpet music to the
    warriors yield?

Harp is hushed within the dark tents and the voice
    of warlike song,
Bards beside the evening camp-fire tales of war do
    not prolong,

Good Yudhishthir's tent is voiceless and my
    brothers look so pale,
Abhimanyu comes not joyous Krishna and his sire
    to hail,

Abhimanyu's love and greeting bless like blessings
    from above,
Fair Subhadra's joy and treasure, Arjun's pride
    and hope and love!"

Softly and with many tear-drops did the sad
    Yudhishthir tell,

DRONA-BADHA

How in dreadful field of battle gallant Abhimanyu
    fell,

How the impious Jayadratha fell on Arjun's
    youthful son,—
He with six proud Kuru chieftains,—Abhimanyu
    all alone,

How the young prince reft of weapon and deprived
    of steel and car,
Fell as falls a Kshatra warrior fighting on the field
    of war!

Arjun heard; the father's bosom felt the cruel
    cureless wound,
"Brave and gallant boy!" he uttered as he sank
    upon the ground,

Moments passed of voiceless sorrow and of
    speechless bitter tear,
Sobs within his mailéd bosom smote the weeping
    listener's ear!

Moments passed; with rising anger quivered
    Arjun's iron frame,
Abhimanyu's cruel murder smote the father's
    heart to flame,

"Didst thou say that Sindhu's monarch on my
 Abhimanyu bore,—
He alone,—and Jayadratha leagued with six
 marauders more,

Didst thou say the impious Kurus stooped unto
 this deed of shame,
Outrage on the laws of honour, stain upon a
 warrior's fame?

Father's curse and warrior's hatred sting them to
 their dying breath,
For they feared my boy in battle, hunted him to
 cruel death,

Hear my vow, benign Yudhishthir, hear me,
 Krishna righteous lord,
Arjun's hand shall slay the slayer, Arjun plights his
 solemn word!

May I never reach the bright sky where the
 righteous fathers dwell,
May I with the darkest sinners live within the
 deepest hell,—

With the men who slay their fathers, shed their
 loving mothers' blood,

DRONA-BADHA

Stain the sacred bed of *gurus*, steal their gold and
  holy food,

Cherish envy, cheat their kinsmen, speak the low
  and dastard lie,—
If, ere comes to-morrow's sunset, Jayadratha doth
  not die,

Jayadratha dies to-morrow, victim to my
  vengeful ire,
Arjun else shall yield his weapons, perish on the
  flaming pyre!"

Softer tear-drops wept the mother, joyless was
  Subhadra's life,—
Krishna's fair and honoured sister, Arjun's dear
  and lovéd wife:

"Dost thou lie on field of battle smeared with dust
  and foeman's gore,
Child of light and love and sweetness whom thy
  hapless mother bore,

Soft thine eye as budding lotus, sweet and gentle
  was thy face,
Are those soft eyes closed in slumber, faded in that
  peerless grace,

And thy limbs so young and tender, on the bare
    earth do they lie,
Where the hungry jackal prowleth and the vulture
    flutters nigh,

Gold and jewels graced thy bosom, gems bedecked
    thy lofty crest,
Doth the crimson mark of sabre decorate that
    manly breast?

Rend Subhadra's stony bosom with a mother's
    cureless grief,
Let her follow Abhimanyu and in death obtain
    relief,

Earth to me is void and cheerless, joyless in my
    hearth and home,
Dreary without Abhimanyu is this weary world
    to roam!

And oh! cheerless is that young heart,
    Abhimanyu's princess-wife,
What can sad Subhadra offer to her joyless
    sunless life,

Close our life in equal darkness, for our day on
    earth is done,

DRONA-BADHA

For our love and light and treasure, Abhimanyu,
   he is gone!"

Long bewailed the anguished mother, fair
   Draupadi tore her hair,
Matsya's princess early widowed shed her young
   heart's blood in tear!

IV
STANDARDS OF THE KURUS: ARJUN'S REVENGE

Morning from the face of battle night's depending
   curtain drew,
Long and shrill his sounding *sankha* then the
   wrathful Arjun blew,

Kurus knew the vow of Arjun, heard the *sankha's*
   deathful blare,
As it rose above the red field, thrilled the startled
   morning air,

"Speed, my Krishna," out spake Arjun, as he held
   aloft his bow,
"For to-day my task is dreadful, cruel is my
   mighty vow!"

THE MAHABHARATA

Fiery coursers urged by Krishna flew with
   lightning's rapid course,
Dashing through the hostile warriors and the
   serried Kuru force,

Brave Durmarsan faced the hero but he strove and
   fought in vain,
Onward thundered Arjun's chariot o'er the dying
   and the slain,

Fierce Duhsasan with his tuskers rushed into the
   line of war,
But the tuskers broke in panic, onward still went
   Arjun's car!

Drona then, the proud preceptor, Arjun's furious
   progress stayed,
Tear-drops filled the eye of Arjun as these gentle
   words he said:

"Pardon, father, if thy pupil shuns to-day thy
   offered war,
'Gainst his Abhimanyu's slayer Arjun speeds his
   battle-car,

Not against my great *acharya* is my wrathful bow-
   string drawn,

DRONA-BADHA

Not against a lovéd father fights a loving
   duteous son!

Heavy on this bleeding bosom sits the darkening
   load of woe,
And an injured father's vengeance seeks the
   slaughtered hero's foe,

Pardon then if sorrowing Arjun seeks a far and
   distant way,
Mighty is the vow of Arjun, cruel is his task
   to-day!"

Passing by the doughty Drona onward sped the
   fiery car,
Through the broken line of warriors, through the
   shattered ranks of war,

Angas and the brave Kalingas vainly crossed his
   wrathful way,
Proud Avantis from the regions where fair
   Chambal's waters stray,

Famed Avanti's fated princes vainly led their
   highland force,
Fell beneath the wrath of Arjun, stayed nor
   stopped his onward course,

Onward still with speed of lightning thundered
　　Arjun's battle-car,
To the spot where Jayadratha stood behind the
　　ranks of war!

Now the sun from highest zenith red and fiery
　　radiance lent,
Long and weary was the passage, Arjun's foaming
　　steeds were spent,

"Arjun!" said the faithful Krishna, "arduous is thy
　　cruel quest,
But thy foaming coursers falter and they need a
　　moment's rest,"

"Be it so," brave Arjun answered, "from our
　　chariot we alight,
Rest awhile the weary horses, Krishna, I will watch
　　the fight!"

Speaking thus the arméd Arjun lightly leaped
　　upon the lea,
Stood on guard with bow and arrow by the green
　　and shady tree,

Krishna groomed the jaded horses, faint and
　　feeble, red with gore,

DRONA-BADHA

With a healing hand he tended wounds the
  bleeding coursers bore,

Watered them beside a river by the zephyrs soft
  caressed,
Gave unto them welcome fodder, gave unto them
  needful rest,

Thus refreshed, the noble coursers Krishna
  harnessed to the car,
And the gleaming fiery Arjun rushed once more to
  fatal war!

Came on him the Kuru warriors, darksome wave
  succeeding wave,
Standards decked with strange devices, streaming
  banners rich and brave,

Foremost was the glorious standard of preceptor
  Drona's son,
Lion's tail in golden brilliance on his battle-chariot
  shone,

Elephant's rope was Karna's ensign made of rich
  and burnished gold,
And a bull bedecked the standard of the bowman
  Kripa bold,

Peacock made of precious metal, decked with
    jewels rich and rare,
Vrishasena's noble standard shone aloft serene
    and fair,

Ploughshare of a golden lustre shining like the
    radiant flame,
Spoke the car of mighty Salya, Madra's king of
    warlike fame,

Far and guarded well by chieftains shone the
    dazzling silver-boar,
Ensign proud of Jayadratha brought from Sindhu's
    sounding shore,

On the car of Somadatta shone a stake of sacrifice,
Silver-boar and golden parrots, these were Salwa's
    proud device,

Last and brightest of the standards, on the prince
    Duryodhan's car,
Lordly elephant in jewels proudly shone above
    the war!

Nine heroic Kuru chieftains, bravest warriors and
    the best,

DRONA-BADHA

Leagued they came to grapple Arjun and on
  faithful Krishna pressed,

Arjun swept like sweeping whirlwind all resistless
  in his force,
Sought no foe and waged no combat, held his ever
  onward course,

For he sighted Jayadratha midst the circling chiefs
  of war,
'Gainst that warrior, grim and silent, Arjun drove
  his furious car!

Now the day-god rolled his chariot on the western
  clouds aflame,
Karna's self and five great chieftains round brave
  Jayadratha came,

Vainly strove the valiant Arjun struggling 'gainst
  the Kuru line,
Charged upon the peerless Karna as he marked
  the day's decline,

Krishna then a prayer whispered; came a friendly
  sable cloud,
Veiled the red sun's dazzling brilliance in a dark
  and inky shroud!

THE MAHABHARATA

Karna deemed the closing darkness now
    proclaimed the close of strife,
Failing in his plighted promise Arjun must
    surrender life,

And his comrade chiefs rejoicing slackened in their
    furious fight,
Jayadratha hailed with gladness thickening shades
    of welcome night!

In that sad and fatal error did the Kuru chiefs
    combine,
Arjun quick as bolt of lightning broke their all
    unguarded line,

Like an onward sweeping wildfire shooting forth
    its lolling tongue,
On the startled Jayadratha, Arjun in his fury flung!

Short the strife; as angry falcon swoops upon its
    helpless prey,
Arjun sped his vengeful arrow and his foeman
    lifeless lay,

Friendly winds removed the dark cloud from the
    reddening western hill,

DRONA-BADHA

And the sun in crimson lustre cast its fiery
    radiance still!

Ere the evening's mantling darkness fell o'er
    distant hill and plain,
Proud Duryodhan's many brothers were by
    vengeful Bhima slain,

And Duryodhan stung by sorrow waged the still
    unceasing fight,
In the thick and gathering darkness torches lit the
    gloom of night!

Karna furious in his anger for his Jayadratha slain,
And for brothers of Duryodhan sleeping lifeless on
    the plain,

'Gainst the gallant son of Bhima drove his deep
    resounding car,
And in gloom and midnight darkness waked the
    echoes of the war!

Bhima's son brave Ghatotkacha twice the steeds of
    Karna slew,
Twice the humbled steedless Karna from the
    dubious battle flew,

Came again the fiery Karna, vengeance flamed
   within his heart,
Like the midnight's lurid lightning sped his fell
   and fatal dart,

Woeful was the hour of darkness, luckless was the
   starry sway,
Bhima's son in youth and valour lifeless on the red
   field lay!

Then was closed the midnight battle, silent shone
   the starry light,
Bhima knew not rest nor slumber through the long
   and woeful night!

V

FALL OF DRONA

Ere the crimson morning glittered proud
   Duryodhan sad at heart,
To the leader of the Kurus did his sorrows thus
   impart:

"Sadly speeds the contest, Drona, on the battle's
   gory plain,

DRONA-BADHA

Kuru chiefs are thinned and fallen and my
    brothers mostly slain,

Can it be, O best of Brahmans, peerless in the art
    of war,
Can it be that we shall falter while thou speed'st
    the battle-car?

Pandu's sons are but thy pupils, Arjun meets thee
    not in fight,
None can face the great *acharya* in his wrath and
    warlike might,

Wherefore then in every battle are the Kuru
    chieftains slain,
Wherefore lie my warlike brothers lifeless on the
    ghastly plain?

Is it that the fates of battle 'gainst the Kuru house
    combine,
Is it that thy heart's affection unto Pandu's sons
    incline?

If thy secret love and mercy still the sons of Pandu
    claim,
Yield thy place to gallant Karna, Anga's prince of
    warlike fame!"

Answered Drona brief and wrathful: "Fair
 Gandhari's royal son,
Reapest thou the gory harvest of thy sinful actions
 done,

Cast no blame in youth's presumption on a
 warrior's fleecy hair,
Faithful unto death is Drona to his promise
 plighted fair!

Ask thyself, O prince Duryodhan, bound by
 battle's sacred laws,
Wherefore fightest not with Arjun for thy house
 and for thy cause,

Ask the dark and deep Sakuni, where is now his
 low device,
Wherefore wields he not his weapon as he wields
 the loaded dice,

Ask the chief who proudly boasted, archer Arjun
 he would slay,
Helméd Arjun sways the battle, whither now doth
 Karna stay?

Know the truth; the gallant Arjun hath no peer on
 earth below,

DRONA-BADHA

And no warrior breathes, Duryodhan, who can
    face thy helméd foe,

Drona knows his sacred duty, and 'tis willed by
    Heaven on high,
Arjun or preceptor Drona shall in this day's
    battle die!"

Now the Sun in crimson splendour rolled his car
    of glistening gold,
Sent his shafts of purple radiance on the plain and
    mountain bold,

And from elephant and charger, from each bravely
    bannered car,
Lighted mailéd kings and chieftains and the
    leaders of the war,

Faced the sun with hands conjoinéd and the
    sacred *mantra* told,—
Hymns by ancient *rishis* chanted, sanctified by
    bards of old!

Worship done, each silent warrior mounted on his
    car or steed,
Onward to the deathful contest did his gallant
    forces lead,

Ill it fared with Pandav forces, doughty Drona
    took the field,
Peer was none midst living warriors of the
    Brahman trained and skilled,

Arjun, faithful to his promise, his preceptor would
    not fight,
King nor chief nor other archer dared to face his
    peerless might.

But old feud like potent poison fires the warrior's
    heart with strife,
Sire to son still unforgotten leaps the hate from
    death to life,

Wrathful princes of Panchala by their deathless
    hatred stung,
Saw their ancient foe in Drona and on him for
    vengeance sprung!

Darkly thought the ancient warrior of the old
    relentless feud,
Fiercely like a jungle-tiger fell upon the hostile
    brood,

Royal Drupad's valiant grandsons in their youth
    untimely slain,

DRONA-BADHA

Victims of a deathless discord, pressed the gory
   battle-plain!

Drupad pale with grief and anger marked his
   gallant grandsons dead
And his army crushed and routed and his bravest
   chieftains fled,

Filled with unforgotten hatred and with father's
   grief and pride,
Rushed the king, and bold Virata charged by
   doughty Drupad's side!

Rose a cry of nameless terror o'er the red and
   ghastly plain,
Noble Drupad, brave Virata, lay among the
   countless slain,

Burning tears the proud Draupadi wept for noble
   father killed,
Maid and matron with their wailing fair Panchala's
   empire filled,

Matsya's joyless widowed princess, for her fate was
   early crost,
Wept with added tears and anguish for her father
   loved and lost!

Waged the war with fearful slaughter, Drona
    onward urged his way
Fate alone and battle's chances changed the
    fortunes of the day,

Aswa-thaman son of Drona was a chief of peerless
    fame,
And an elephant of battle bore that chieftain's
    warlike name,

And that proud and lordly tusker Bhima in his
    prowess slew,
Rank to rank from friend to foeman then a garbled
    message flew:

"Aswa-thaman son of Drona is by mighty Bhima
    slain,"
Drona heard that fatal message, bent his
    anguished head in pain!

"Speak Yudhishthir, soul of virtue!" thus the proud
    preceptor cried,
"Thou in truth hast never faltered and thy lips
    have never lied,

Speak of valiant Aswa-thaman, Drona's hope and
    pride and joy,

DRONA-BADHA

Hath he fallen in this battle, is he slain, my
    gallant boy,

Feeble are the hands of Drona and his prowess
    quenched and gone,
Fleecy are his ancient tresses and his earthly task
    is done!"

Said Yudhishthir thus in answer: "Tusker Aswa-
    thaman's dead,"
Drona heard but half the accents, feebly drooped
    his sinking head,

Then the prince of fair Panchala swiftly drove
    across the plain,
Marked his father's cruel slayer, marked his noble
    father slain!

Dhrista-dyumna bent his weapon and his shaft
    was pointed well,
And the priest and proud preceptor, peerless
    Drona lifeless fell,

And the fatal day was ended, Kurus fled in abject
    fear,
Arjun for his ancient teacher dropped a silent
    filial tear!

Book X
Karna-Badha
(*Fall of Karna*)

Karna was chosen as the leader of the Kuru forces after the death of Drona, and held his own for two days. The great contest between Karna and Arjun, long expected and long deferred, came on at last. It is the crowning incident of the Indian Epic, as the contest between Hector and Achilles is the crowning incident of the Iliad. With a truer artistic skill than that of Homer, the Indian poet represents Karna as equal to Arjun in strength and skill, and his defeat is only due to an accident.

After the death of Karna, Salya led the Kuru troops on the eighteenth and last day of the war, and fell. A midnight slaughter in the Pandav camp, perpetrated by the vengeful son of Drona, concludes the war. Duryodhan, left wounded by Bhima, heard of the slaughter and died happy.

Books viii., ix., and x. of the original have been abridged in this Book.

I
KARNA AND ARJUN MEET

Sights of red and ghastly carnage day disclosed upon the plain,
Mighty chiefs and countless warriors round the warlike Drona slain,

Sad Duryodhan gazed in sorrow and the tear was in his eye,
Till his glances fell on Karna and his warlike heart beat high!

"Karna!" so exclaimed Duryodhan, "hero of resistless might,
Thou alone canst serve the Kuru in this dread and dubious fight,

Step forth, Kuru's chief and leader, mount thy sounding battle-car,
Lead the still unconquered Kurus to the trophies of the war!

Matchless was the ancient Bhishma in this famed and warlike land,

KARNA-BADHA

But a weakness for Yudhishthir palsied Bhishma's
slaying hand,

Matchless too was doughty Drona in the warrior's
skill and art,
Kindness for his pupil Arjun lurked within the
teacher's heart!

Greater than the ancient grandsire, greater than
the Brahman old,
Fiercer in thy deathless hatred, stronger in thy
prowess bold,

Peerless Karna, lead us onward to a brighter
happier fate,
For thy arm is nerved to action by an unforgotten
hate!

Lead us as the martial SKANDA led the conquering
gods of old,
Smite the foe as angry INDRA smote the Danavs
fierce and bold,

As before the light of morning flies the baleful
gloom of night,
Pandavs and the proud Panchalas fly before thy
conquering might!"

THE MAHABHARATA

Priests with hymns and chanted *mantra* and with
every sacred rite
Hailed him Leader of the Kurus, chieftain of
unconquered might,

Earthen jars they placed around him with the
sacred water full,
Elephant's tusk they laid beside him and the horn
of mighty bull,

Gem and jewel, corn and produce, by the arméd
hero laid,
Silken cloth of finest lustre o'er his crownéd head
they spread,

Brahmans poured the holy water, bards his lofty
praises sung,
Kshatras, Vaisyas, purer Sudras hailed him Leader
bold and strong!

"Vanquish warlike sons of Pritha!" thus the holy
Brahmans blessed,
Gold and garments, food and cattle, joyous Karna
on them pressed,

And the holy rite concluded, Karna ranged his
men in war,

KARNA-BADHA

To the dreaded front of battle drove his swift and
 conquering car!

Morn to noon and noon to evening raged the
 battle on the plain,
Countless warriors fought and perished, car-borne
 chiefs were pierced and slain,

Helméd Arjun, crownéd Karna, met at last by will
 of fate,
Life-long was their mutual anger, deathless was
 their mutual hate!

And the firm earth shook and trembled 'neath the
 furious rush of war,
And the echoing welkin answered shouts that
 nations heard afar,

And the thickening cloud of arrows filled the
 firmament on high,
Darker, deeper, dread and deadlier, grew the
 angry face of sky,

Till the evening's sable garment mantled o'er the
 battle-field,
And the angry rivals parted, neither chief could
 win or yield!

II
FALL OF KARNA

At the break of morning Karna unto Prince
 Duryodhan went,
Thus in slow and measured accents to his inner
 thoughts gave vent:

"Morning dawns, O Kuru's monarch! mighty
 Arjun shall be slain,
Or fulfilling warrior's duty Karna dyes the gory
 plain!

Long through life within our bosoms ever burnt
 the mutual hate,
Oft we met and often parted, rescued by the will
 of fate,

But yon sun with crimson lustre sees us meet to
 part no more,
Gallant Arjun's course this evening or proud
 Karna's shall be o'er,

Room is none for Arjun's glory and for archer
 Karna's fame,

KARNA-BADHA

One must sink and one must sparkle with a
  brighter richer flame!

List yet more; in wealth of arrows and in wondrous
  strength of bow,
Arjun scarcely me surpasseth, scarcely I excel
  my foe,

In the light skill of the archer and in sight and
  truth of aim,
Arjun beats not, scarcely rivals, Karna's proud and
  peerless fame!

If his wondrous bow *Gandiva* is the gift of gods in
  heaven,
Karna's bow the famed *Vijaya* is by Par'su-Rama
  given,

Ay, the son of Jamadagni, kings of earth who
  proudly slayed,
On the youthful arms of Karna his destructive
  weapon laid!

Yet I own, O king of Kuru! Arjun doth his foe
  excel,—
Matchless are his fiery coursers, peerless Krishna
  leads them well,

THE MAHABHARATA

Krishna holds the reins for Arjun, Krishna speeds
 his battle-car,
Drives the lightning-wingéd coursers o'er the
 startled field of war,

Sweeps in pride his sounding chariot till it almost
 seems to fly,
Arjun lords it o'er the battle like the comet in
 the sky!

Grant me, monarch, mighty Salya drive my swift
 and warlike steed,
And against the car-borne Arjun, Karna's fiery
 chariot lead,

Salya too is skilled, like Krishna, with the steed
 and battle-car,
Equal thus I meet my foeman in this last and
 fatal war!"

Spake Duryodhan; warlike Salya mounted Karna's
 sounding car,
Karna sought for mighty Arjun in the serried ranks
 of war:

"Hundred milch-kine Karna offers, costly
 garment, yellow gold,

KARNA-BADHA

Unto him who in this battle points to me my
    foeman bold,

Cars and steeds and fertile acres, peaceful hamlets
    rich and fair,
Dark-eyed damsels lotus-bosomed, crowned with
    glossy raven hair,

These are his who points out Arjun hiding from
    this fatal war,
Arjun's snowy steeds and banner and his swift and
    thund'ring car!"

Karna spake, but long and loudly laughed the king
    of Madra's land,
As he reined the fiery coursers with his strong and
    skillful hand,

"Of rewards and gifts," he uttered, "little need is
    there, I ween,
Arjun is not wont to tarry from the battle's
    glorious scene,

Soon will Arjun's snowy coursers shake the battle's
    startled field,
Helméd Arjun like a comet gleams with bow and
    sword and shield!

As the forest-ranging tiger springs upon his fated
    prey,
As the hornéd bull infuriate doth the weakling
    cattle slay,

As the fierce and lordly lion smites the timid
    jungle-deer,
Arjun soon shall smite thee, Karna, for he knows
    not dread nor fear,

Save thee then, O mighty archer! While I drive my
    sounding car,
Pandu's son hath met no equal in the valiant art
    of war!"

Darkly frowned the angry Karna, Salya held the
    loosened rein,
Dashing through the hostile forces then the
    warrior sped amain,

Through the serried ranks of battle Karna drove in
    furious mood,
Facing him in royal splendour good Yudhishthir
    fearless stood!

Surging ranks of brave Nishadas closed between
    and fought in vain,

KARNA-BADHA

Proud Panchalas stout and faithful vainly strove
    among the slain,

Onward came the fiery Karna like the ocean's
    heaving swell,
With the sweeping wrath of tempest on the good
    Yudhishthir fell!

Wrathful then the son of Pandu marked his
    noblest chieftains dead,
And in words of scornful anger thus to archer
    Karna said:

"Hast thou, Karna, vowed the slaughter of my
    younger Arjun brave,
Wilt thou do Duryodhan's mandate, proud
    Duryodhan's willing slave,

Unfulfilled thy vow remaineth, for the righteous
    gods ordain,
By Yudhishthir's hand thou fallest, go and slumber
    with the slain!"

Fiercely drew his bow Yudhishthir, fiercely was the
    arrow driven,
Rocky cliff or solid mountain might the shaft have
    pierced and riven,

THE MAHABHARATA

Lightning-like it came on Karna, struck and
    pierced him on the left,
And the warrior fell and fainted as of life and sense
    bereft!

Soon he rose; the cloud of anger darkened o'er his
    livid face,
And he drew his godlike weapon with a more than
    godlike grace,

Arrows keen and dark as midnight gleaming in
    their lightning flight,
Struck Yudhishthir's royal armour with a fierce
    resistless might!

Clanking fell the shattered armour from his person
    fair and pale,
As from sun's meridian splendour clouds are
    drifted by the gale,

Armourless but bright and radiant brave
    Yudhishthir waged the fight,
Bright as sky with stars bespangled on a clear and
    cloudless night,

And he threw his pointed lances like the summer's
    bursting flood,

KARNA-BADHA

Once again Yudhishthir's weapons drank his fiery
   foeman's blood!

Pale with anguish, wrathful Karna fiercely turned
   the tide of war,
Cut Yudhishthir's royal standard, crushed his
   sumptuous battle-car,

And he urged his gallant coursers till his chariot
   bounding flew,
And with more than godlike prowess then his
   famed *Vijaya* drew,

Faint Yudhishthir sorely bleeding waged no more
   the fatal fight,
Carless, steedless, void of armour, sought his
   safety in his flight!

"Speed, thou timid man of penance!" thus
   insulting Karna said,
"Famed for virtue not for valour! blood of thine I
   will not shed,

Speed and chant thy wonted *mantra*, do the rites
   that sages know,
Bid the helmèd warrior Arjun come and meet his
   warlike foe!"

To his tent retired Yudhishthir in his wrath and in his shame,
Spake to Arjun who from battle to his angry elder came:

"Hast thou yet, O tardy Arjun, base insulting Karna slain,
Karna dealing dire destruction on this battle's reddened plain?

Like his teacher Par'su-Rama dyes in purple blood his course,
Like a snake of deathful poison Karna guards the Kuru force,

Karna smote my chariot-driver and my standard rent in twain,
Shattered car and lifeless horses strew the red inglorious plain,

Scarce with life in speechless anguish from the battle-field I fled,
Scorn of foes and shame of kinsmen! Warrior's fame and honour dead!

Ten long years and three Yudhishthir joy nor peace nor rest hath seen,

KARNA-BADHA

And while Karna lives and glories all our insults
    still are green,

Hast thou, Arjun, slain that chieftain as in swelling
    pride he stood,
Hast thou wiped our wrongs and insults in that
    chariot-driver's blood?"

"At a distance," Krishna answered, "fiery Arjun
    fought his way,
Now he seeks the archer Karna and he vows his
    death to-day."

Anger lit Yudhishthir's forehead and a tremor
    shook his frame,
As he spake to silent Arjun words of insult and of
    shame:

"Wherefore like a painted warrior doth the helméd
    Arjun stand,
Wherefore useless lies *Gandiva* in his weak and
    nerveless hand,

Wherefore hangs yon mighty sabre from his belt of
    silk and gold,
Wherefore doth the peerless Krishna drive his
    coursers fleet and bold,

THE MAHABHARATA

If afar from war's arena timid Arjun seeks to hide,
If he shuns the mighty Karna battling in
   unconquered pride?

Arjun! yield thy famed *Gandiva* unto worthier
   hands than thine,
On some braver, truer warrior let thy mighty
   standard shine,

Yield thy helmet and thy armour, yield thy
   gleaming sword and shield,
Hide thee from this deathful battle, matchless
   Karna rules the field!"

Sparkled Arjun's eye in anger with a red and livid
   flame,
And the tempest of his passion shook his more
   than mortal frame,

Heedless, on the sword-hilt Arjun placed his swift
   and trembling hand,
Heedless, with a warrior's instinct drew the dark
   and glistening brand!

Sacred blood of king and elder would have stained
   his trenchant steel,

KARNA-BADHA

But the wise and noble Krishna strove the fatal
    feud to heal:

"Not before thy elder, Arjun, but in yonder purple
    field,
'Gainst thy rival and thy foeman use thy warlike
    sword and shield,

Render honour to thy elder, quench thy hasty
    impious wrath,
Render faith to holy *sastra*, leave not virtue's
    sacred path,

Bow before thy virtuous elder as before the gods
    in heaven,
Sheathe thy sword and quell thy passion, be thy
    hasty sin forgiven!"

Duteous Arjun silent listened and obeyed the
    mandate high,
Tears of manly sorrow trickled from his soft and
    altered eye,

Dear in joy and dear in suffering, calm his
    righteous elder stood,
Dear in Indra-prastha's mansions, dearer in the
    jungle wood!

Arjun sheathed his flashing sabre, joined his hands
  and hung his head,
Fixed his eye on good Yudhishthir and in humble
  accents said:

"Pardon, great and saintly monarch, vassal's
  disrespectful word,
Pardon, elder, if a younger heedless drew his sinful
  sword,

But thy hest to yield my weapon stung my soul to
  bitter strife,
Dearer is the bow *Gandiva* unto Arjun than
  his life,

Pardon if the blood of anger mantled o'er this
  rugged brow,
Pardon if I drew my sabre 'gainst my duty and
  my vow,

For that hasty act repenting Arjun bows thy heart
  to move,
Grant me, holy king and elder, monarch's grace
  and brother's love!"

From Yudhishthir's altered eyelids gentle tears of
  sorrow start,

KARNA-BADHA

And he lifts his younger brother to his ever-loving
 heart:

"Arjun, I have wronged thee brother, and no fault
 or sin is thine,
Hasty words of thoughtless anger 'scaped these
 sinful lips of mine,

Bitter was my shame and anguish when from
 Karna's car I fled,
Redder than my bleeding bosom warrior's fame
 and honour bled,

Hasty words I uttered, Arjun, by my pain and
 anguish driven,
Wipe them with a brother's kindness, be thy elder's
 sin forgiven!"

Stronger by his elder's blessing Arjun mounts the
 battle-car,
Krishna drives the milk-white coursers to the
 thickening ranks of war.

Onward came the fiery Karna with his chiefs and
 arméd men,
Salya urged his flying coursers with the whip and
 loosened rein,

THE MAHABHARATA

Often met and often parted, life-long rivals in
    their fame,
Not to part again the heroes, each before the
    other came,

Not to part until a chieftain by the other chief was
    slain,
Arjun dead or lifeless Karna pressed the Kuru-
    kshetra plain!

Long they strove, but neither archer could his
    gallant foeman beat,
Though like surging ocean billows did the angry
    warriors meet,

Arjun's arrows fell on Karna like the summer's
    angry flood,
Karna's shafts like hissing serpents drank the
    valiant Arjun's blood,

Fierce and quick from his *Gandiva* angry accents
    Arjun woke,
Till the bow-string strained and heated was by
    sudden impulse broke!

"Hold," cried Arjun to his rival, "mind the
    honoured rules of war,

KARNA-BADHA

Warriors strike not helpless foemen thus disabled
on the car,

Hold, brave Karna, until Arjun mends his over-
strainéd bow,
Arjun then will crave for mercy not from god nor
mortal foe!"

Vain he spake, for wild with anger heedless Karna
fiercely lowered,
Thick and fast on bowless Arjun countless arrows
darkly showered,

Like the cobra dark and hissing Karna's gleaming
lightning dart,
Struck the helpless archer Arjun on his broad and
bleeding heart!

Furious like a wounded tiger quivering in the
darksome wood,
With his mended warlike weapon now the angry
Arjun stood,

Blazing with a mighty radiance like a flame in
summer night,
Fierce he fell on archer Karna with his more than
mortal might!

Little recked the dauntless Karna if his foe in
 anger rose,
Karna feared not face of mortal, dreaded not
 immortal foes,

Nor with all his wrath and valour Arjun conquered
 him in war,
Till within the soft earth sinking stuck the wheel of
 Karna's car!

Stood unmoved the tilted chariot, vainly wrathful
 Salya strove,
Urging still the struggling coursers Karna's heavy
 car to move,

Vainly too the gallant Karna leaped upon the
 humid soil,
Sought to lift the sunken axle with a hard
 unwonted toil,

"Hold," he cried to noble Arjun, "wage no false
 and impious war
On a foeman, helpless, carless,—thou upon thy
 lofty car."

Loudly laughed the helméd Arjun, answer nor
 rejoinder gave,

KARNA-BADHA

Unto Karna pleading virtue Krishna answered
    calm and grave:

"Didst thou seek the path of virtue, mighty Karna,
    archer bold,
When Sakuni robbed Yudhishthir of his empire
    and his gold,

Didst thou tread the path of honour on
    Yudhishthir's fatal fall,
Heaping insults on Draupadi in Hastina's
    council hall?

Didst thou then fulfil thy duty when, Yudhishthir's
    exile crost,
Krishna asked in right and justice for Yudhishthir's
    empire lost,

Didst thou fight a holy battle when with six
    marauders skilled,
Karna hunted Abhimanyu and the youthful hero
    killed?

Speak not then of rules of honour, blackened in
    your sins you die,
Death is come in shape of Arjun, Karna's fatal
    hour is nigh!"

Stung to fury and to madness, faint but frantic Karna fought,
Reckless, ruthless, and relentless, valiant Arjun's life he sought,

Sent his last resistless arrow on his foeman's mighty chest,
Arjun felt a shock of thunder on his broad and mailéd breast!

Fainting fell the bleeding Arjun, darkness dimmed his manly eye,
Pale and breathless watched his warriors, anxious watched the gods in sky,

Then it passed, and helméd Arjun rose like newly lighted fire,
Abhimanyu's sad remembrance kindled fresh a father's ire!

And he drew his bow *Gandiva*, aimed his dart with stifled breath,
Vengeance for his murdered hero winged the fatal dart of death,

Like the fiery bolt of lightning Arjun's lurid arrow sped,

KARNA-BADHA

Like a rock by thunder riven Karna fell among the
    dead!

III
FALL OF SALYA

Darkly closed the shades of midnight, Karna still
    and lifeless lay,
Ghast and pale o'er slaughtered thousands fell the
    morning's sickly ray,

Bowman brave and proud preceptor Kripa to
    Duryodhan said,
Tear bedimmed the warrior's eyelids and his
    manly bosom bled:

"Leaderless are Kuru's forces by a dire misfortune
    crost,
Like the moonless shades of midnight in their
    utter darkness lost,

Like a summer-dried river, weary waste of arid
    sand,
Lost its pride of fresh'ning waters sweeping o'er
    the grateful land!

As a spark of fire consumeth summer's parched
　　and sapless wood,
Kuru's lordless, lifeless forces shall be angry
　　Arjun's food,

Bhima too shall seek fulfillment of the dreadful
　　vow he made,
Brave Satyaki wreak his vengeance for his sons
　　untimely slayed!

Bid this battle cease, Duryodhan, pale and fitful is
　　thy star,
Blood enough of friendly nations soaks this
　　crimson field of war,

Bid them live,—the few survivors of a vast and
　　countless host,
Let thy few remaining brothers live,—for many are
　　the lost,

Kindly heart hath good Yudhishthir, still he seeks
　　for rightful peace,
Render back his ancient kingdom, bid this war of
　　kinsmen cease!"

"Kripa," so Duryodhan answered, "in this sad and
　　fatal strife,

KARNA-BADHA

Ever foremost of our warriors, ever careless of
    thy life,

Ever in the council chamber thou hast words of
    wisdom said,
Needless war and dire destruction by thy peaceful
    counsel stayed,

Every word thou speakest, Kripa, is a word of
    truth and weight,
Nathless thy advice for concord, wise preceptor,
    comes too late!

Hope not that the good Yudhishthir will again our
    friendship own,
Cheated once by deep Sakuni of his kingdom and
    his throne,

Rugged Bhima will not palter, fatal is the vow
    he made,
Vengeful Arjun will not pardon gallant Abhimanyu
    dead!

Fair Draupadi doth her penance, so our ancient
    matrons say,
In our blood to wash her insult and her proud
    insulters slay,

Fair Subhadra morn and evening weeps her dear
    departed son,
Feeds Draupadi's deathless anger for the hero
    dead and gone,

Deeply in their bosoms rankle wrongs and insults
    we have given,
Blood alone can wash it, Kripa, such the cruel will
    of Heaven!

And the hour for peace is over, for our best sleep
    on the plain,
Brothers, kinsmen, friends, and elders slumber
    with the countless slain,

Shall Duryodhan like a recreant now avoid the
    deathful strife,
After all his bravest warriors have in war
    surrendered life,

Shall he, sending them to slaughter, now survive
    and learn to flee,
Shall he, ruler over monarchs, learn to bend the
    servile knee?

Proud Duryodhan sues no favour even with his
    dying breath,

KARNA-BADHA

Unsubdued and still unconquered, changeless
    even unto death,

Salya valiant king of Madra leads our arméd hosts
    to-day,
Or to perish or to conquer, gallant Kripa, lead
    the way!"

Meanwhile round the brave Yudhishthir calmly
    stood the Pandav force,
As the final day of battle now began its fatal
    course,

"Brothers, kinsmen, hero-warriors," so the good
    Yudhishthir said,
"Ye have done your share in battle, witness
    countless foemen dead

Sad Yudhishthir is your eldest, let him end this
    fatal strife,
Slay the last of Kuru chieftains or surrender
    throne and life!

Bold Satyaki ever faithful with his arms protects
    my right,
Drupad's son with watchful valour guards my left
    with wonted might,

THE MAHABHARATA

In the front doth Bhima battle, careful Arjun
    guards the rear,
I will lead the battle's centre which shall know not
    flight nor fear!"

Truly on that fatal morning brave Yudhishthir kept
    his word,
Long and fiercely waged the combat with fair
    Madra's valiant lord,

Thick and fast the arrows whistled and the lances
    pointed well,
Till with crashing sound of thunder Salya's mighty
    standard fell!

Rescued by the son of Drona, Salya rushed again
    to war,
Slew the noble milk-white coursers of
    Yudhishthir's royal car,

And as springs the hungry lion on the spotted
    jungle-deer,
Salya rushed upon Yudhishthir reckless and
    unknown to fear!

Brave Yudhishthir marked him coming and he
    hurled his fatal dart,

KARNA-BADHA

Like the fatal curse of Brahman sank the weapon
    in his heart,

Blood suffused his eye and nostril, quivered still
    his feeble hand,
Like a cliff by thunder riven Salya fell and shook
    the land!

Ended was the fatal battle, for the *Mlechcha* king
    was slain,
Pierced by angry Sahadeva false Sakuni pressed
    the plain,

All the brothers of Duryodhan tiger-waisted
    Bhima slew,
Proud Duryodhan pale and panting from the field
    of battle flew!

IV
NIGHT OF SLAUGHTER: DURYODHAN'S DEATH

Far from battle's toil and slaughter, by a dark and
    limpid lake,
Sad and slow and faint Duryodhan did his humble
    shelter take,

THE MAHABHARATA

But the valiant sons of Pandu with the hunter's
  watchful care,
Thither tracked their fallen foeman like a wild
  beast in its lair!

"Gods be witness," said Duryodhan, flaming in his
  shame and wrath,
"Boy to manhood ever hating we have crossed
  each other's path,

Now we meet to part no longer, proud Duryodhan
  fights you all,
Perish he, or sons of Pandu, may this evening see
  your fall!"

Bhima answered: "For the insults long endured
  but not forgiven,
Me alone you fight, Duryodhan, witness righteous
  gods in heaven,

Call to mind the dark destruction planned of old
  in fiendish ire,
In the halls of Varnavata to consume us in the fire,

Call to mind the scheme deceitful, deep Sakuni's
  dark device,

KARNA-BADHA

Cheating us of fame and empire by the trick of loaded dice,

Call to mind that coward insult and the outrage foul and keen,
Flung on Drupad's saintly daughter and our noble spotless queen,

Call to mind the stainless Bhishma for thy sins and folly slain,
Lifeless proud preceptor Drona, Karna lifeless on the plain,

Perish in thy sins, Duryodhan, perish too thy hated name,
And thy dark life crime-polluted ends, Duryodhan, in thy shame!"

Like two bulls that fight in fury blind with wounds and oozing blood,
Like two wild and warring tuskers shaking all the echoing wood,

Like the thunder-wielding INDRA, YAMA monarch of the dead,
Dauntless Bhima and Duryodhan fiercely strove and fought and bled!

THE MAHABHARATA

Sparks of fire shot from their maces and their faces
    ran with blood,
Neither won and neither yielded, matched in
    strength the rivals stood,

Till his vow remembered Bhima, and he raised his
    weapon high,
With a foul attack but fatal broke Duryodhan's
    shattered knee!

Through the sky a voice resounded as the great
    Duryodhan fell,
And the earth the voice re-echoed o'er her distant
    hill and dale,

Beasts and birds in consternation flew o'er land
    and azure sky,
Men below and heavenly *Siddhas* trembled at the
    fatal cry!

Darkness fell upon the battle, proud Duryodhan
    dying lay,
But the slaughter of the combat closed not with
    the closing day,

Ancient feud and hatred linger after battle's
    sweeping flood,

KARNA-BADHA

And the father's deathless anger courseth in the
    children's blood,

Drona slept and gallant Drupad, for their earthly
    task was done,
Vengeance fired the son of Drona 'gainst the royal
    Drupad's son!

Sable shadows of the midnight fell o'er battle's
    silent plain,
Faintly shone the fitful planets on the dying and
    the slain,

And the vengeful son of Drona fired by omens
    dark and dread,
Stole into the tents of foemen with a soft and
    noiseless tread!

Dhrista-dyumna and Sikhandin, princes of
    Panchala's land,
Fell beneath the proud avenger Aswa-thaman's
    reeking hand,

Ay, where Drupad's sleeping grandsons, fair
    Draupadi's children lay,
Stole the cruel arm of vengeance, smothered them
    ere dawn of day!

Done the ghastly work of slaughter, Aswa-thaman
    bent his way
Where beside the limpid waters lone Duryodhan
    dying lay,

And Duryodhan blessed the hero with his feeble
    fleeting breath,
Joy of vengeance cheered his bosom and he died a
    happy death!

Book XI
Sraddha
(*Funeral Rites*)

The death of Duryodhan concludes the war, and it is followed by the lament of women and the funerals of the deceased warriors. The passages translated in this Book form Section x., portions of Sections xvi., xvii., and xxvi., and the whole of Section xxvii. of Book xi. of the original text.

I
KURU WOMEN VISIT THE BATTLE-FIELD

Spake the ancient Dhrita-rashtra, father of a
   hundred sons,
Sonless now and sorrow-stricken, dark his ebbing
   life-tide runs:

"Gods fulfil my life's last wishes! Henchmen, yoke
   my royal car,
Dhrita-rashtra meets his princes in the silent field
   of war,

Speed unto the Queen Gandhari, to the dames of
   Kuru's house,
To each dear departed warrior wends his fair and
   faithful spouse!"

Queen Gandhari sorrow-laden with the ancient
   Pritha came,
And each weeping widowed princess and each
   wailing childless dame,

And they saw the hoary monarch, father of a
   perished race,

SRADDHA

Fresh and loud awoke their sorrow, welling tears
    suffused their face,

Good Vidura ever gentle whispered comfort
    unto all,
Placed the dames within their chariots, left
    Hastina's palace hall!

Loud the wail of woe and sorrow rose from every
    Kuru house,
Children wept beside their mothers for each
    widowed royal spouse,

Veilèd dwellers of the palace, scarce the gods their
    face had seen,
Heedless now through mart and city sped each
    widowed childless queen,

From their royal brow and bosom gem and jewel
    cast aside,
Loose their robes and loose their tresses, quenched
    their haughty queenly pride!

So when falls the antlered monarch, struck by woe
    and sudden fear
Issuing from their snowy mountains listless stray
    the dappled deer,

THE MAHABHARATA

So when smit by sudden panic, milk-white mares
  that scour the plain,
Wildly toss their flowing tresses, shake their soft
  and glossy mane!

Clinging to her weeping sister wept each dame in
  cureless pain,
For the lord the son or father in the deathful battle
  slain,

Wept and smote her throbbing bosom and in bitter
  anguish wailed,
Till her senses reeled in sorrow, till her woman's
  reason failed!

Veiléd queens and bashful maidens, erst they
  shunned the public eye,
Blush nor shame suffused their faces as they
  passed the city by,

Gentle-bosomed, kindly hearted, erst they wiped
  each other's tear,
Now by common sorrow laden knew no sister's
  words of cheer!

With this troop of wailing women, deep in woe,
  disconsolate,

SRADDHA

Slow the monarch of the Kurus passed Hastina's
   outer gate,

Men from stall and loom and anvil, men of every
   guild and trade,
Left the city with the monarch, through the open
   country strayed,

And a universal sorrow filled the air and
   answering sky,
As when ends the mortal's *Yuga* and the end of
   world is nigh!

II

GANDHARI'S LAMENT FOR THE SLAIN

Stainless Queen and stainless woman, ever
   righteous ever good,
Stately in her mighty sorrow on the field Gandhari
   stood!

Strewn with skulls and clotted tresses, darkened by
   the stream of gore,
With the limbs of countless warriors is the red
   field covered o'er,

Elephants and steeds of battle, car-borne chiefs
 untimely slain,
Headless trunks and heads dissevered fill the red
 and ghastly plain,

And the long-drawn howl of jackals o'er the scene
 of carnage rings,
And the vulture and the raven flap their dark and
 loathsome wings.

Feasting on the blood of warriors foul *Pisachas* fill
 the air,
Viewless forms of hungry *Rakshas* limb from limb
 the corpses tear!

Through this scene of death and carnage was the
 ancient monarch led,
Kuru dames with faltering footsteps stepped
 amidst the countless dead,

And a piercing wail of anguish burst upon the
 echoing plain,
As they saw their sons or fathers, brothers, lords,
 amidst the slain,

As they saw the wolves of jungle feed upon the
 destined prey,

SRADDHA

Darksome wanderers of the midnight prowling in
    the light of day!

Shriek of pain and wail of anguish o'er the ghastly
    field resound,
And their feeble footsteps falter and they sink
    upon the ground,

Sense and life desert the mourners as they faint in
    common grief,
Death-like swoon succeeding sorrow yields a
    moment's short relief!

Then a mighty sigh of anguish from Gandhari's
    bosom broke,
Gazing on her anguished daughters unto Krishna
    thus she spoke:

"Mark my unconsoléd daughters, widowed queens
    of Kuru's house,
Wailing for their dear departed, like the osprey for
    her spouse!

How each cold and fading feature wakes in them a
    woman's love,
How amidst the lifeless warriors still with restless
    steps they rove,

THE MAHABHARATA

Mothers hug their slaughtered children all
 unconscious in their sleep,
Widows bend upon their husbands and in
 ceaseless sorrow weep,

Mighty Bhishma, hath he fallen, quenched is
 archer Karna's pride,
Doth the monarch of Panchala sleep by foeman
 Drona's side?

Shining mail and costly jewels, royal bangles strew
 the plain,
Golden garlands rich and burnished deck the
 chiefs untimely slain,

Lances hurled by stalwart fighters, clubs of mighty
 wrestlers killed,
Swords and bows of ample measure, quivers still
 with arrows filled!

Mark the unforgotten heroes, jungle prowlers 'mid
 them stray,
On their brow and mailéd bosoms heedless perch
 the birds of prey,

Mark the great unconquered heroes famed on
 earth from west to east,

SRADDHA

Kankas perch upon their foreheads, hungry wolves
    upon them feast!

Mark the kings, on softest cushion scarce the
    needed rest they found,
Now they lie in peaceful slumber on the hard and
    reddened ground,

Mark the youths who morn and evening listed to
    the minstrel's song,
In their ear the loathsome jackal doth his doleful
    wail prolong!

See the chieftains with their maces and their
    swords of trusty steel,
Still they grasp their tried weapons,—do they still
    the life-pulse feel?"

III
GANDHARI'S LAMENT FOR DURYODHAN

Thus to Krishna, Queen Gandhari strove her
    woeful thoughts to tell,
When, alas, her wandering vision on her son
    Duryodhan fell,

THE MAHABHARATA

Sudden anguish smote her bosom and her senses
    seemed to stray,
Like a tree by tempest shaken senseless on the
    earth she lay!

Once again she waked in sorrow, once again she
    cast her eye
Where her son in blood empurpled slept beneath
    the open sky,

And she clasped her dear Duryodhan, held him
    close unto her breast,
Sobs convulsive shook her bosom as the lifeless
    form she prest,

And her tears like rains of summer fell and washed
    his noble head,
Decked with garlands still untarnished, graced
    with *nishkas* bright and red!

"'Mother!' said my dear Duryodhan when he went
    unto the war,
'Wish me joy and wish me triumph as I mount the
    battle-car,'

'Son!' I said to dear Duryodhan, 'Heaven avert a
    cruel fate,

SRADDHA

Yato dharma stato jayah! Triumph doth on Virtue
wait!'

But he set his heart on battle, by his valour wiped
his sins,
Now he dwells in realms celestial which the
faithful warrior wins,

And I weep not for Duryodhan, like a prince he
fought and fell,
But my sorrow-stricken husband, who can his
misfortunes tell!

Ay! my son was brave and princely, all resistless in
the war,
Now he sleeps the sleep of warriors, sunk in gloom
his glorious star,

Ay! my son 'mid crownéd monarchs held the first
and foremost way,
Now he rests upon the red earth, quenched his
bright effulgent ray,

Ay! my son the best of heroes, he hath won the
warrior's sky,
Kshatras nobly conquer, Krishna, when in war
they nobly die!

Hark the loathsome cry of jackals, how the wolves
 their vigils keep,
Maidens rich in song and beauty erst were wont to
 watch his sleep,

Hark the foul and blood-beaked vultures flap their
 wings upon the dead,
Maidens waved their feathery *pankhas* round
 Duryodhan's royal bed,

Peerless bowman! mighty monarch! nations still
 his hests obeyed,
As a lion slays a tiger, Bhima hath Duryodhan
 slayed!

Thirteen years o'er Kuru's empire proud
 Duryodhan held his sway,
Ruled Hastina's ancient city where fair Ganga's
 waters stray,

I have seen his regal splendour with these ancient
 eyes of mine,
Elephants and battle-chariots, steeds of war and
 herds of kine,

Kuru owns another master and Duryodhan's day
 is fled,

SRADDHA

And I live to be a witness! Krishna, O that I were
dead!

Mark Duryodhan's noble widow, mother proud of
Lakshman bold,
Queenly in her youth and beauty, like an altar of
bright gold,

Torn from husband's sweet embraces, from her
son's entwining arms,
Doomed to life-long woe and anguish in her youth
and in her charms,

Rend my hard and stony bosom crushed beneath
this cruel pain,
Should Gandhari live to witness noble son and
grandson slain?

Mark again Duryodhan's widow, how she hugs his
gory head,
How with gentle hands and tender softly holds
him on his bed,

How from dear departed husband turns she to her
dearer son,
And the tear-drops of the mother choke the
widow's bitter groan,

Like the fibre of the lotus tender-golden is her frame,
O my lotus! O my daughter! Bharat's pride and Kuru's fame!

If the truth resides in *Vedas*, brave Duryodhan dwells above,
Wherefore linger we in sadness severed from his cherished love,

If the truth resides in *Sastra*, dwells in sky my hero son,
Wherefore linger we in sorrow since their earthly task is done?"

IV

FUNERAL RITE

Victor of a deathful battle, sad Yudhishthir viewed the plain,
Friends and kinsmen, kings and chieftains, countless troops untimely slain,

And he spake to wise Sudharman pious priest of Kuru's race,

SRADDHA

Unto Sanjay, unto Dhaumya, to Vidura full of grace,

Spake unto the brave Yuyutsu, Kuru's last surviving chief,
Spake to faithful Indrasena and to warriors sunk in grief:

"Pious rites are due to foemen and to friends and kinsmen slain,
None shall lack a fitting funeral, none shall perish on the plain."

Wise Vidura and his comrades sped on sacred duty bound,
Sandalwood and scented aloes, fragrant oil and perfumes found,

Silken robes of costly splendour, fabrics by the artist wove,
Dry wood from the thorny jungle, perfume from the scented grove,

Shattered cars and splintered lances, hewed and ready for the fire,
Piled and ranged in perfect order into many a funeral pyre.

Kings and princes, noble warriors, were in rank and order laid,
And with streams of fragrant *ghrita* were the rich libations made,

Blazed the fire with wondrous radiance by the rich libations fed,
Sanctifying and consuming mortal remnants of the dead.

Brave Duryodhan and his brothers, Salya of the mighty car,
Bhurisravas king of nations, Jayadratha famed in war,

Abhimanyu son of Arjun, Lakshman proud Duryodhan's son,
Somadatta and the Srinjays famed for deeds of valour done,

Matsya's monarch proud Virata, Drupad fair Panchala's king,
And his sons, Panchala's princes, whose great deeds the minstrels sing,

Cultured monarch of Kosala and Gandhara's wily lord,

SRADDHA

Karna proud and peerless archer, matchless with
 his flaming sword,

Bhagadatta eastern monarch all resistless in
 his car,
Ghatotkacha son of Bhima, Alambusha famed
 in war,

And a hundred other monarchs all received the
 pious rite,
Till the radiance of the fire-light chased the
 shadows of the night!

Pitri-medha due to fathers was performed with
 pious care,
Hymns and wails and lamentations mingled in the
 midnight air,

Sacred songs of *rik* and *saman* rose with women's
 piercing wail,
And the creatures of the wide earth heard the
 sound subdued and pale,

Smokeless and with radiant lustre shone each red
 and lighted pyre,
Like the planets of the bright sky throbbing with
 celestial fire!

THE MAHABHARATA

Men in nations, countless, nameless, from each
> court and camp afar,
From the east and west collected, fell in Kuru-
> Kshetra's war,

Thousand fires for them were lighted, they
> received the pious rite,
Such was good Yudhishthir's mandate, such was
> wise Vidura's might,

All the dead were burned to ashes and the sacred
> rite was o'er,
Dhrita-rashtra and Yudhishthir slowly walked to
> Ganga's shore!

V

OBLATION TO KARNA

Sacred Ganga, ample-bosomed, sweeps along in
> regal pride,
Rolling down her limpid waters through high
> banks on either side,

Childless dames and weeping widows thither in
> their anguish came,

SRADDHA

Due and holy rites to render to departed chiefs
 of fame,

Casting forth their jewelled girdles, gems and
 scarfs belaced with gold,
Gave oblations of the water unto warriors true
 and bold,

Unto fathers, unto husbands, unto sons in battle
 slayed,
Offerings of the sacred water sorrowing wives and
 mothers made.

And so great the host of mourners wending to
 perform the rite,
That their footsteps made a pathway in the sad
 and sacred site,

And the shelving banks of Ganga, peopled by the
 sorrowing train,
Wide-expanding, vast and sealike, formed a scene
 of woe and pain!

But a wave of keener sorrow swept o'er Pritha's
 heaving breast,
As unto her weeping children thus her secret she
 expressed:

*"He, my sons, the peerless bowman, mighty in his
   battle-car,*
*Who by will of fate untimely was by Arjun slain
   in war,*

*He whom as the son of Radha, chariot-driver ye have
   thought,*
*But who shone with SURYA'S lustre as his countless
   foes he fought,*

*He who faced your stoutest warriors and in battle never
   failed,*
*Bravely led the Kuru forces and in danger never
   quailed,*

*He who knew no peer in prowess, owned in war no
   haughtier name,*
*Yielded life but not his honour and by death hath
   conquered fame,*

*He in truth who never faltered, never left his vow
   undone,*
Offer unto him oblation, Karna was my eldest son!

*Karna was your honoured elder and the Sun inspired
   his birth,*

SRADDHA

*Karna in his rings and armour Sun-like trod the
    spacious earth!"*

Pritha spake; the Pandav brothers groaned in
    penitence and pain,
And they wept in woe and anguish for the brother
    they had slain,

Hissing forth his sigh of anguish like a crushed
    and wounded snake,
Sad Yudhishthir to his mother thus his inward
    feelings spake:

"Didst thou, mother, bear the hero fathomless like
    ocean dread,
Whose unfailing glistening arrows like its countless
    billows sped,

Didst thou bear that peerless archer all-resistless
    in his car,
Sweeping with the roar of ocean through the
    shattered ranks of war?

Didst thou hide the mighty warrior, mortal man of
    heavenly birth,
Crushing 'neath his arm of valour all his foemen
    on the earth,

Didst thou hide the birth and lineage of that chief
 of deathful ire,
As a man in folds of garments seeks to hide the
 flaming fire?

Arjun wielder of *Gandiva* was for us no truer stay
Than was Karna for the Kurus in the battle's
 dread array,

Monarchs matched not Karna's glory nor his
 deeds of valour done,
Midst the mighty car-borne warriors mightiest
 warrior Karna shone!

Woe to us! our eldest brother we have in the battle
 slain,
And our nearest dearest elder fell upon the gory
 plain,

Not the death of Abhimanyu from the fair
 Subhadra torn,
Not the slaughter of the princes by the proud
 Draupadi borne,

Not the fall of friends and kinsmen and Panchala's
 mighty host,

SRADDHA

Like thy death afflicts my bosom, noble Karna
    loved and lost!

Monarch's empire, victor's glory, all the treasures
    earth can yield,
Righteous bliss and heavenly gladness, harvest of
    the heavenly field,

All that wish can shape and utter, all that nourish
    hope and pride,
All were ours, O noble Karna, hadst thou rested
    by our side,

And this carnage of the Kurus these sad eyes had
    never seen,
Peace had graced our blessed empire, happy would
    the earth have been!"

Long bewailed the sad Yudhishthir for his elder
    loved and dead,
And oblation of the water to the noble Karna
    made,

And the royal dames of Kuru viewed the sight with
    freshening pain,
Wept to see the good Yudhishthir offering to his
    brother slain,

And the widowed queen of Karna with the women
    of his house
Gave oblations to her hero, wept her loved and
    slaughtered spouse!

Done the rites to the departed, done oblations to
    the dead,
Slowly then the sad survivors on the river's margin
    spread,

Far along the shore and sandbank of the sacred
    sealike stream
Maid and matron lave their bodies 'neath the
    morning's holy beam,

And ablutions done, the Kurus slow and sad and
    cheerless part,
Wend their way to far Hastina with a void and
    vacant heart.

Book XII
Aswa-Medha
(*Sacrifice of the Horse*)

The real Epic ends with the war and the funerals of the deceased warriors. Much of what follows in the original Sanscrit poem is either episodical or comparatively recent interpolation. The great and venerable warrior Bhishma, still lying on his deathbed, discourses for the instruction of the newly crowned Yudhishthir on various subjects like the Duties of Kings, the Duties of the Four Castes, and the Four Stages of Life. He repeats the discourses of other saints, of Bhrigu and Bharadwaja, of Manu and Brihaspati, of Vyasa and Suka, of Yajnavalkya and Janaka, of Narada and Narayana. He explains *Sankhya* philosophy and *Yoga* philosophy, and lays down the laws of Marriage, the laws of Succession, the rules of Gifts, and the rules of Funeral Rites. He preaches the cult of Krishna, and narrates endless legends, tales, traditions, and myths about sages and saints, gods and mortal kings. All this is told in two Books containing about twenty-two thousand couplets, and forming nearly one-fourth of the entire Sanscrit Epic!

The reason of adding all this episodical and comparatively recent matter to the ancient Epic is not far to seek. The Epic became more popular with the nation at large than dry codes of law and philosophy, and generations of Brahmanical writers laboured therefore to insert in the Epic itself their rules of caste and moral conduct, their laws and philosophy. There is no more venerable character in the Epic than Bhishma, and these rules and laws have therefore been supposed to come from his lips on the solemn occasion of his death. As a storehouse of Hindu laws and traditions and moral rules these episodes are invaluable; but they form no part of the real Epic, they are not a portion of the leading story of the Epic, and we pass them by.

Bhishma dies and is cremated; but the endless exposition of laws, legends, and moral rules is not yet over. Krishna himself takes up the task in a new Book, and, as he has done once before in the *Bhagavat-gita*, he now once more explains to Arjun in the *Anu-gita* the great truths about Soul and Emancipation, Creation and the Wheel of Life, True Knowledge and Rites and Penance. The adventures of the sage Utanka, whom Krishna meets, then take up a good many pages. All this forms no part of the real Epic, and we pass it by.

ASWA-MEDHA

Yudhishthir has in the meantime been crowned king of the Kurus at Hastinapura, and a posthumous child of Abhimanyu is named Parikshit, and is destined to succeed to the throne of the Kurus. But Yudhishthir's mind is still troubled with the thoughts of the carnage of the war, of which he considers himself guilty, and the great saint Vyasa advises the performance of the *aswamedha*, or the Sacrifice of the Horse, for the expiation of the sin.

The Sacrifice of the Horse was an ancient Hindu custom practised by kings exercising suzerain powers over surrounding kings. A horse was let free, and was allowed to wander from place to place, accompanied by the king's guard. If any neighbouring king ventured to detain the animal, it was a signal for war. If no king ventured to restrain the wanderer, it was considered a tacit mark of submission to the owner of the animal. And when the horse returned from its peregrinations, it was sacrificed with great pomp and splendour at a feast to which all neighbouring kings were invited.

Yudhishthir allowed the sacrificial horse to wander at will, and Arjun accompanied it. Wherever the horse was stopped, Arjun fought and conquered, and thus proclaimed the supremacy of Yudhishthir over all neighbouring potentates. After various wars and adventures in various regions,

Arjun at last returned victorious with the steed to Hastinapura, and the sacrifice commenced.

The description of the sacrifice is somewhat artificial, and concerns itself with rites and ceremonious details and gifts to Brahmans, and altogether bears unmistakable evidence of the interpolating hand of later priestly writers. Nevertheless we cannot exclude from this translation of the leading incidents of the Epic the last great and crowning act of Yudhishthir, now anointed monarch of Kuruland.

The portion translated in this Book forms Sections lxxxv. and parts of Sections lxxxviii. and lxxxix. of Book xiv. of the original text.

I
THE GATHERING

Victor of a hundred battles, Arjun bent his
    homeward way,
Following still the sacred charger free to wander as
    it may,

Strolling minstrels to Yudhishthir spake of the
    returning steed,
Spake of Arjun wending homeward with the
    victor's crown of meed,

And they sang of Arjun's triumphs in Gandhara's
    distant vale,
On the banks of Brahmaputra and in Sindhu's
    rocky dale.

Twelfth day came of *Magha's* bright moon and
    auspicious was the star,
Nigher came the victor Arjun from his conquests
    near and far,

Good Yudhishthir called his brothers, faithful
    twins and Bhima true,

Spake to them in gentle accents, and his words
    were grave and few:

"Bhima! Now returneth Arjun with the steed from
    many a fray,
So they tell me, noble brother, who have met him
    on the way,

And the time of *aswa-medha* day by day is drawing
    nigh,
Magha's full moon is approaching, and the winter
    passeth by,

Let the Brahmans versed in *Vedas* choose the
    sacrificial site,
For the feast of many nations, for the *aswa-medha*
    rite."

Bhima heard of Arjun's coming,—hero with the
    curly hair,—
And to do Yudhishthir's mandate did with
    gladsome heart repair,

Brahmans versed in sacrifices, cunning architects
    of fame,
Builders of each various altar with the son of
    Pritha came,

ASWA-MEDHA

And upon a level greensward measured forth the
    sacred site,
Laid it out with halls and pathways for the
    sacrificial rite.

Mansions graced with gem and jewel round the
    bright arena shone,
Palaces of golden lustre glinted in the
    morning sun,

Gilt and blazoned with devices lofty columns
    stood around,
Graceful arches gold-surmounted spanned the
    consecrated ground,

Gay pavilions rose in beauty round the
    sacrificial site,
For the queens of crownéd monarchs wending to
    the holy rite,

Humbler dwellings rose for Brahmans, priests of
    learning and of fame,
Come to view Yudhishthir's *yajna* and to bless
    Yudhishthir's name.

Messengers with kindly greetings went to
    monarchs far-renowned,

Asked them to Hastina's city, to the consecrated ground,

And to please the great Yudhishthir came each king and chieftain bold,
With their slaves and dark-eye damsels, arms and horses, gems and gold,

Came and found a royal welcome in pavilions rich and high,
And the sealike voice of nations smote the echoing vault of sky!

With his greetings did Yudhishthir, for each chief and king of men,
Cooling drinks and sumptuous viands, beds of regal pride ordain,

Stables filled with corn and barley and with milk and luscious cane
Greeted tall and warlike tuskers and the steeds with flowing mane.

Munis from their hermitages to the sacred *yajna* came,
Rishis from the grove and forest lisping BRAHMA'S holy name,

ASWA-MEDHA

Famed *Acharyas* versed in *Vedas* to the city held
  their way,
Brahmacharins with grass-girdle, chanting sweet
  the *saman* lay,

Welcomed Kuru's pious monarch, saint and sage
  and man of grace,
And with gentle condescension showed each priest
  his fitting place.

Skilled mechanics, cunning artists, raised the
  structures for the rite,
And with every needful object graced the
  sacrificial site,

Every duty thus completed, joyful Yudhishthir's
  mind,
And he blessed his faithful brothers with an elder's
  blessings kind.

II
THE FEASTING

Men in nations are assembled, hymns are sung by
  saint and sage,
And in learnéd disputations keen disputants oft
  engage,

And the concourse of the monarchs view the
  splendour of the rite,
Like the glorious sky of INDRA is the sacrificial
  site!

Bright festoons and flaming streamers are on
  golden arches hung,
Groups of men and gay-dressed women form a
  bright and joyous throng,

Jars of cool and sparkling waters, vessels rich with
  gold inlaid,
Costly cups and golden vases are in order due
  arrayed.

Sacrificial stakes of timber with their golden
  fastenings graced,

ASWA-MEDHA

Consecrated by the *mantra* are in sumptuous order
    placed,

Countless creatures of the wide earth, fishes from
    the lake and flood,
Buffaloes and bulls from pasture, beasts of prey
    from jungle wood,

Birds and every egg-born creature, insects that
    from moisture spring,
Denizens of cave and mountain for the sacrifice
    they bring.

Noble chiefs and mighty monarchs gaze in wonder
    on the site,
Filled with every living object, corn and cattle for
    the rite,

Curd and cake and sweet confection are for
    feasting Brahmans spread,
And a hundred thousand people are with
    sumptuous viands fed!

With the accents of the rain-cloud drum and
    trumpet raise their voice,
Speak Yudhishthir's noble bounty, bid the sons of
    men rejoice,

Day by day the holy *yajna* grows in splendour and in joy,
Rice in hillocks feeds all comers, maid and matron, man and boy,

Lakes of curd and lakes of butter speak Yudhishthir's bounteous feast,
Nations of the Jambu-dwipa share it, greatest and the least!

For a hundred diverse races from a hundred regions came,
Ate of good Yudhishthir's bounty, sang of good Yudhishthir's fame,

And a thousand proud attendants, gay with earrings, garland-graced,
Carried food unto the feeders and the sweet confections placed,

Viands fit for crownéd monarchs were unto the Brahmans given,
Drinks of rich and cooling fragrance like the nectar-drink of heaven!

III
SACRIFICE OF ANIMALS

Victor of a hundred battles, Arjun came with
 conquering steed,
Vyasa herald of the *Vedas* bade the holy rite
 proceed:

"For the day is come, Yudhishthir, let the sacrifice
 be done,
Let the priests repeat the *mantra* golden as the
 morning sun!

Threefold bounteous be thy presents and a
 threefold merit gain,
For thy wealth of gold is ample, be thy gifts like
 summer's rain,

May the threefold rich performance purify the
 darkening stain,
Blood of warriors and of kinsmen slaughtered on
 the gory plain,

May the *yajna's* pure ablution wash thee of the
 cruel sin,

THE MAHABHARATA

And the meed of sacrificers may the good
   Yudhishthir win!"

Vyasa spake; and good Yudhishthir took the *diksha*
   of the rite,
And commenced the *aswa-medha* gladdening every
   living wight,

Round the altar's holy lustre moved the priests
   with sacred awe,
Swerved not from the rule of duty, failed not in the
   sacred law.

Done the rite of pure *pravargya* with the pious
   hymn and lay,
To the task of *abhishava* priests and Brahmans led
   the way,

And the holy Soma-drinkers pressed the sacred
   Soma plant,
And performed the pure *savana* with the solemn
   saman chant.

Bounty waits on squalid hunger, gifts dispel the
   suppliant's fear,
Gold revives the poor and lowly, mercy wipes the
   mourner's tear,

ASWA-MEDHA

Tender care relieves the stricken by the gracious
    king's command,
Charity with loving sweetness spreads her smile
    o'er all the land!

Day by day the *aswa-medha* doth with sacred rites
    proceed,
Day by day on royal bounty poor and grateful
    myriads feed,

And adept in six *Vedangas*, strict in vow and rich
    in lore,
Sage preceptors, holy teachers, grew in virtue
    ever more!

Six good stakes of *vilwa* timber, six of hard *khadira*
    wood,
Six of seasoned *sarvavarnin*, on the place of *yajna*
    stood,

Two were made of *devadaru*, pine that on Himalay
    grows,
One was made of wood of *slesha*, which the
    sacrificer knows,

Other stakes of golden lustre quaint with curious
    carving done,

Draped in silk and gold-brocaded like the
constellations shone!

And the consecrated altar built and raised of
bricks of gold,
Shone in splendour like the altar Daksha built in
days of old,

Eighteen cubits square the structure, four deep
layers of brick in height,
With a spacious winged triangle like an eagle in its
flight!

Beasts whose flesh is pure and wholesome,
dwellers of the lake or sky,
Priests assigned each varied offering to each
heavenly power on high,

Bulls of various breed and colour, steeds of mettle
true and tried,
Other creatures, full three hundred, to the many
stakes were tied.

Deva-rishis viewed the feasting, sweet *Gandharvas*
woke the song,
Apsaras like gleams of sunlight on the greensward
tripped along,

ASWA-MEDHA

Kinnaras and *Kim-purushas* mingled in the
 holy rite,
Siddhas of austerest penance stood around the
 sacred site,

Vyasa's great and gifted pupils who the holy
 hymns compiled,
Helped the royal *aswa-medha*, on the royal *yajna*
 smiled!

From the bright ethereal mansions heavenly
 minstrel Narad came,
Chitra-sena woke the music, singer of celestial
 fame,

Cheered by more than mortal music priests their
 holy task begun,
And Yudhishthir's fame and virtue with a brighter
 lustre shone!

IV

SACRIFICE OF THE HORSE

Birds and beasts were immolated for the sacrificial
 food,

Then before the sacred charger priests in rank and
 order stood,

And by rules of *Veda* guided slew the horse of
 noble breed,
Placed Draupadi, *Queen of yajna*, by the slain and
 lifeless steed,

Hymns and gifts and deep devotion sanctified the
 noble Queen,
Woman's true and stainless virtue, woman's worth
 and wisdom keen!

Priests adept in sacred duty cooked the steed with
 pious rite,
And the steam of welcome fragrance sanctified the
 sacred site,

Good Yudhishthir and his brothers, by the rules by
 rishis spoke,
Piously inhaled the fragrance and the sin-
 destroying smoke!

Severed limbs and sacred fragments of the courser
 duly dressed,
Priests upon the blazing altar as a pious offering
 placed,

ASWA-MEDHA

Vyasa herald of the *Vedas* raised his voice in holy
    song,
Blessed Hastina's righteous monarch and the
    many-nationed throng!

V

GIFTS

Unto Brahmans gave Yudhishthir countless *nishkas*
    of bright gold,
Unto sage and saintly Vyasa all his realm and
    wealth untold,

But the bard and ancient *rishi* who the holy *Vedas*
    spake,
Rendered back the monarch's present, earthly gift
    he might not take!

"Thine is Kuru's ancient empire, rule the nations
    of the earth,
Gods have destined thee as monarch from the
    moment of thy birth,

Gold and wealth and costly present let the priests
    and Brahmans hoard,

Be it thine to rule thy subjects as their father and
   their lord!

Krishna too in gentle accents to the doubting
   monarch said:
"Vyasa speaketh word of wisdom and his mandate
   be obeyed!"

From the *rishi* good Yudhishthir then received the
   Kuru-land,
With a threefold gift of riches gladdened all the
   priestly band,

Pious priests and grateful nations to their distant
   regions went,
And his share of presents Vyasa to the ancient
   Pritha sent.

Fame and virtue Kuru's monarch by the *aswa-
   medha* wins,
And the rite of pure ablution cleanses all
   Yudhishthir's sins,

And he stands amid his brothers, brightly
   beaming, pure and high,
Even as INDRA stands encircled by the dwellers of
   the sky,

And the concourse of the monarchs grace
    Yudhishthir's regal might,
As the stars and radiant planets grace the stillness
    of the night!

Gems and jewels in his bounty, gold and garments
    rich and rare,
Gave Yudhishthir to each monarch, slaves and
    damsels passing fair,

Loving gifts to dear relations gave the king of
    righteous fame,
And the grateful parting monarchs blessed
    Yudhishthir's hallowed name.

Last of all with many tear-drops Krishna mounts
    his lofty car,
Faithful still in joy or sorrow, faithful still in peace
    or war,

Arjun's comrade, Bhima's helper, good
    Yudhishthir's friend of yore,
Krishna leaves Hastina's mansions for the sea-girt
    Dwarka's shore!

Conclusion

The real Epic ends with the war and with the funerals of the deceased warriors, as we have stated before, and Yudhishthir's Horse-Sacrifice is rather a crowning ornament than a part of the solid edifice. What follows the sacrifice is in no sense a part of the real Epic; it consists merely of concluding personal narratives of the heroes who have figured in the poem.

Dhrita-rashtra retires into a forest with his queen Gandhari, and Pritha, the mother of the Pandav brothers, accompanies them. In the solitude of the forest the old Dhrita-rashtra sees as in a vision the spirits of all the slain warriors, his sons and grandsons and kinsmen, clad and armed as they were in battle. The spirits disappear in the morning at the bidding of Vyasa, who had called them up. At last Dhrita-rashtra and Gandhari and Pritha are burnt to death in a forest conflagration, death by fire being considered holy.

Krishna at Dwarka meets with strange and tragic adventures. The Vrishnis and the Andhakas become irreligious and addicted to drinking, and fall a prey to internal dissensions. Valadeva and

Krishna die shortly after, and the city of the Yadavas is swallowed up by the ocean.

Then follow the two concluding Books of the Epic, the *Great Journey* and the *Ascent to Heaven*, so beautifully rendered into English by Sir Edwin Arnold. On hearing of the death of their friend Krishna, the Pandav brothers place Prakshit, the grandson of Arjun, on the throne, and retire to the Himalayas. Draupadi drops down dead on the way, then Sahadeva, then Nakula, then Arjun, and then Bhima. Yudhishthir alone proceeds to heaven in person in a celestial car.

There Yudhishthir undergoes some trial, bathes in the celestial Ganges, and rises with a celestial body. He then meets Krishna, now in his heavenly form, blazing in splendour and glory. He meets his brothers whom he had lost on earth, but who are now Immortals in the sky, clad in heavenly forms. INDRA himself appears before Yudhishthir, and introduces him to others who were dear to him on earth, and are dear to him in heaven. Thus speaks INDRA to Yudhishthir:

"This is She the fair Immortal! Her no human
   mother bore,
Sprung from altar as Draupadi human shape for
   thee she wore,

CONCLUSION

By the Wielder of the Trident she was waked to
   form and life,
Born in royal Drupad's mansion, righteous man,
   to be thy wife,

These are bright aërial beings, went for thee to
   lower earth,
Borne by Drupad's stainless daughter as thy
   children took their birth!

This is monarch Dhrita-rashtra who doth o'er
   Gandharvas reign,
This is peerless archer Karna, erst on earth by
   Arjun slain,

Like the Sun in ruddy splendour, for the Sun
   inspired his birth,
As the son of chariot-driver he was known upon
   the earth!

'Midst the *Sadhyas* and the *Maruts*, 'midst
   Immortals pure and bright,
Seek thy friends the faithful Vrishnis matchless in
   their warlike might.

Seek and find the brave Satyaki who upheld thy
   cause so well,

THE MAHABHARATA

Seek the Bhojas and Andhakas who in Kuru-
 kshetra fell!

This is gallant Abhimanyu whom the fair
 Subhadra bore,
Still unconquered in the battle, slain by fraud in
 yonder shore,

Abhimanyu son of Arjun, wielding Arjun's peerless
 might,
With the Lord of Night he ranges, beauteous as
 the Lord of Night!

This, Yudhishthir, is thy father, by thy mother
 joined in heaven,
Oft he comes into my mansions in his flowery
 chariot driven.

This is Bhishma stainless warrior, by the *Vasus* is
 his place,
By the god of heavenly wisdom teacher Drona sits
 in grace!

*These and other mighty warriors in the earthly battle
 slain,*
*By their valour and their virtue walk the bright
 ethereal plain,*

CONCLUSION

*They have cast their mortal bodies, crossed the radiant
   gate of heaven,*
For to win celestial mansions unto mortals it is given,

*Let them strive by kindly action, gentle speech,
   endurance long,—*
*Brighter life and holier future unto sons of men
   belong!"*

Glossary

ABHISHAVA, a religious rite.

ABHISHEKA, sacred ablution.

ACHARYA, preceptor.

AJYA, a form of sacrificial offering.

APSARA, celestial nymph.

ARGHYA, an offering due to an honoured guest.

ARYA, an honourable person, an Aryan.

ASRAM, hermitage.

ASURA, demon, enemies of gods.

ASWAMEDHA, a horse-sacrifice.

BAIDURYA, lapis-lazuli.

BRAHMACHARIN, one who has taken vows and lives an austere life.

CHANDAN, sandal-tree; also the fragrant sandal paste.

CHOWRI (*properly* CHAMARI), the yak, the tail of which is used as a fan.

DASAPUTRA, son of a slave.

DEVA, gods.

DEVADARU (*lit.* heavenly tree), the Himalayan pine.

GLOSSARY

DEVA-KANYA, celestial maid.
DEVA-RISHI, celestial saint.
DHARMA-RAJA, monarch by reason of piety and virtue.
DIKSHA, initiation into a sacred rite.

GANDHARVA, celestial musician.
GANDIVA, Arjun's bow.
GHRITA or GHEE, clarified butter.
GURU, preceptor.

HOMA, a sacrificial rite or offering.
HOWDA, the seat on an elephant.

IDA, a form of sacrificial offering.

KANKA, a bird of prey.
KHADIRA, a tree, a kind of acacia.
KINNARA, a fabulous being with the body of a man and the face of a horse, the counterpart of the Greek Centaur.
KOKIL, an Indian bird answering to the English cuckoo, and prized for its sweet note.

MAGHA, a winter month.
MAHUT or MAHAMATRA, elephant driver.

GLOSSARY

MANTRA, hymn, incantation.

MLECHCHA, outer barbarian. All who were not Hindus were designated by this name.

MUNI, saint, anchorite.

NAGA, snake; a being of the lower or snake world; also a tribe in Eastern India.

NISHADA, an aboriginal race.

NISHKA, a coin, often used as ornament.

NULLAH, a rivulet or rill.

PANKHA (from Sanscrit *paksha*, wing), a fan.

PITRI-MEDHA, sacrifice and offering due to departed ancestors.

PRAVARGYA, a religious rite.

PURANA, ancient and sacred chronicles.

PURUSHA, the soul.

RAJASUYA, an imperial sacrifice.

RAKSHA, a class of fabulous beings represented as demons and night-rangers, and wearing various shapes at will. The inhabitants of Ceylon, with whom the hero of the Epic fought, are represented as Rakshas.

RIK, hymn recited at sacrifice.

RISHI, saint or anchorite.

GLOSSARY

SAMADHI, austere religious practice.

SAMAN, hymn chanted at sacrifice.

SAMI, a dark leafy tree.

SANKHA, conch shell used as a sounding instrument in wars and in festivities.

SARVAVARNIN, an Indian tree.

SASTRA, sacred scriptures.

SAVANA, a religious rite.

SAVITRI, a hymn; also the goddess of the hymn.

SIDDHA, holy celestial beings.

SLESHA, an Indian tree.

SRI, the goddess of beauty and wealth, wife of Vishnu.

SUPARNA, celestial bird.

SWAYAMVARA, a form of bridal, the bride selecting her husband from among suitors.

TIRTHA, holy rites at the crossing of rivers.

TRIRATRA, a three nights' penance and fast.

VEDA, the most ancient and holiest scriptures of the Hindus.

VIJAYA, Karna's bow.

VILWA, a tree bearing an edible fruit.

VINA, the lyre.

GLOSSARY

YAJNA, sacrifice.

YATO DHARMA STATO JAYAH, 'where there is virtue there is victory'.

YOJANA, a measure of distance equal to about nine English miles.

YUGA, the period of the world's existence.

MACMILLAN COLLECTOR'S LIBRARY

Own the world's great works of literature in one beautiful collectible library

Designed and curated to appeal to book lovers everywhere, Macmillan Collector's Library editions are small enough to travel with you and striking enough to take pride of place on your bookshelf. These much-loved literary classics also make the perfect gift.

Beautifully made, every Macmillan Collector's Library book adheres to the same high production values. Each hardback features gilt edges, a ribbon marker and cloth binding, and every paperback has a bespoke illustrated cover.

Discover a new and exciting anthology or cherish your favourite classic stories with this elegant collection.

Macmillan Collector's Library: own, collect, and treasure

Discover the full range at
panmacmillan.com/mcl